THE MAKEOVER

MATT MCGREGOR

INKUBATOR
BOOKS

Published by Inkubator Books
www.inkubatorbooks.com

Copyright © 2024 by Matt McGregor

ISBN (eBook): 978-1-83756-449-1
ISBN (Paperback): 978-1-83756-450-7
ISBN (Hardback): 978-1-83756-451-4

PROLOGUE

The police are here much faster than I expected.

I'm standing at the edge of the forest above that ridiculous house, watching their lights flashing in the dark. There's an army of them—not just the locals, but state police and several unmarked cars.

Dozens of cops and detectives, all trying to piece together how it happened. They'll come up with a story soon enough. It will be the story I want them to believe.

An ambulance arrives, not that it will be of any use. I made sure to finish the job.

I'm almost shocked to see what I've done. So many lives have been completely shattered, all because of me.

I pull my bag from behind the rotten log and change my clothes. Then I take out the small trowel and dig through the snow.

After a minute, the trowel falls to the ground, and I find that I'm weeping. What's wrong with me? Everything went perfectly. Once the police have finished their investigation,

I'll have the money I need. I can take care of my mother, give her the life she always wanted—and then be free.

Grieve not. Find strength in what remains behind.

I wipe my eyes, then dig until I reach the frozen ground. I stuff in the bloodied clothes and pack the snow in tight. I'll come back later and burn everything, but there's no time to do it now. I need to leave the state as quickly as I can.

As I'm packing down the hole, I think I hear a voice behind me.

I turn, but there's no one there. My heart is racing. I could have sworn it was him—the man I killed.

I suppose this will be my fate: To always mistake the rustle of leaves for the whispers of ghosts.

But who cares? I'm free, and that's all I ever wanted.

Now, I can finally live.

1

VIRGINIA

"**A**re you sure you know what you're doing?"

Richard ignores me. We're 500 feet in the air, following the threads of a braided river deeper into the mountains.

I know it's beautiful—but at that moment, I don't care. I'm gripping my seat so hard I worry my nails will snap off.

The helicopter suddenly lifts and swings back along the face of the mountain. I let out an involuntary squeal and wonder, not for the first time, how my seatbelt will help when we explode into the rocks below.

"That's our cabin."

I smile at the way he says it. *Our cabin.* Though we've been married for two years, I still don't really believe I have a share in everything he owns. In New York, we'd been living in his Upper West Side apartment, driving his BMW, living off his salary.

I didn't even have to work—not that I had much of a career before we met. I'm a 30-year-old communications assistant with a BA from a state school. Sometimes, I feel less like his wife than a charity case, some unfortunate urchin he's adopted off the streets.

I crane my neck and see a small house set against the mountain. Though it's only October, there's already a dusting of snow around the property.

"You never told me about this."

"I'm a man of mystery," he says with a grin.

I laugh. Richard is anything but a man of mystery; more like a creature of habit. For the years I've known him, he's followed the same routine. The gym at five, followed by eggs at a cafe. At his desk at seven-thirty. Chicken salad for lunch. Salmon or steak for dinner. Home by seven, asleep by ten.

Until recently, sex once a week—always on Friday nights. No alcohol. And most definitely no drugs.

"I wonder what other surprises you have in store."

He swings the helicopter around and begins our descent. I squeal again, and he laughs. In my headphones, it sounds harsh, like he's mocking me. I tell myself I'm just being sensitive, something Mom told me a million times growing up.

But the truth is, for the last few months, all of our conversations have had this same simmering hostility.

"No more surprises," he says. "Just a fresh start."

It's no one's fault, but I'm determined to make it right. When he suggested we move to his family ranch in Montana, I thought this could be my lifeline. Maybe once we were away from the routines of Manhattan, the long work days, and the dinner parties, we'd be able to resuscitate our dying marriage.

He loves me—I'm sure of that. I catch his astonished glances sometimes. When we were first married, he would whisper beautiful phrases in my ear during sex, snatches of my favorite poems. I wonder if he'll ever do that again.

"That's our place."

I look down at a vast property nestled against the hills. On the eastern side, I can see herds of cattle grazing. Horses, too, and a small house near the road. That's where we will be living. A few hundred feet away, close to the pine forest at the edge of the property, is a mansion built in the style of an old English country house, plopped absurdly onto the Montana landscape.

Richard tells me that it hasn't been lived in for over twenty years. The builders are currently modernizing everything, but when the renovations are finished, it will be our home.

A dozen bedrooms, multiple living rooms and bathrooms.

Ours.

"I love it," I say, and I mean it. Growing up in Queens, I didn't spend much time in nature. Maybe out here, I can become a different person. Perhaps we can become a different couple, too.

He's not the problem. He's everything I need in a husband. He's sober, stable, and kind. He's barely ever raised his voice at me. And he's a great provider. As an early employee at a now-massive engineering firm, he's a millionaire many times over.

I'm the problem, I sing in my head. I need to change.

I must make this marriage work, as if my life depends on it.

Because, in some ways, it does.

2

VIRGINIA

"You didn't need to do that," I say as we walk across the tarmac of the small private airport near the town of Frostwood. "We could have just driven from Kalispell."

Richard waves at a disheveled old man with a white beard and a cowboy hat. "Yeah, but where's the fun in that?"

"I never knew you were such an adrenaline junkie. When did you even learn how to pilot a helicopter?"

"Air Force," he grunts. "I did a tour in Iraq, remember?"

"Sorry," I say. Over the two years of our marriage, he has only mentioned his time in Iraq a handful of times and never in any detail. "Didn't know you flew helicopters."

"I was a different person back then," he says quietly.

"Well… thanks."

There's an awkward silence. I've become used to them over the last few months, but I'm glad when he yells out, "PJ!" and grips the disheveled man's hand like he's an old friend. "This is my wife, Virginia. Virginia, PJ is our ranch manager. He's been looking after the property for decades."

"Property manager and chauffeur, apparently," PJ grunts before pointing to a beat-up pickup truck. "There's the chariot."

"And our belongings?" Richard asks.

"All arrived this morning. Got a couple of guys to unpack everything. Should feel right at home."

I get in the back seat with Richard, trying not to visibly wrinkle my nose at the smell of grass and cow shit. We drive north, through the resort town of Frostwood, towards the mountains. There are glaciers only a few miles away, but down here, the weather is still mild. That would all change by Christmas. When the heavy snow came in the new year, the place would be even more packed with tourists visiting the ski fields nearby.

"It's pretty," I say to break the silence. "Must have been a nice place to grow up."

"I wouldn't know," Richard replies, and I kick myself. I had forgotten that Richard didn't grow up here. Richard's father got his mother pregnant at college. She dropped out while he transferred to a college in another state, abandoning them both. Richard grew up in poverty, and under the pressure of raising a kid on her own, his mom became addicted to heroin. It was only when his dad died, at eighteen, that Richard found himself inheriting the entire estate.

"Good for kids, bad for teens," PJ chimes in from the front. "We've got our fair share of delinquents around here."

My phone vibrates in my pocket. I check the message, then immediately click the screen off.

"Who was that?"

"Mom," I lie, as PJ turns off the main road into a driveway. "Eastman Estate? That's pretty fancy."

"Yeah. My grandfather always thought this place was special. More than just a ranch, anyway."

I hold my tongue, though the sign—along with the mansion his grandfather has built—is about the most pretentious thing I've ever seen. Who were these people, deciding to act like English aristocrats in the foothills of the Rockies?

We park by a small wooden house surrounded by freshly mown grass. As soon as we get out, a border collie bounds across the field and jumps up at me.

"Hey, girl," I laugh as the dog licks my face. I've always loved dogs. As a kid, my best friend was a French bulldog that we called Manny, but he died when I was thirteen. Back then, I had dreams of becoming a vet, though my hippy, artsy Mom quickly quashed any interest I had in the sciences.

I scratch her ears, and she leaps up at me again, placing her paws on my chest. "What's your name?"

"Casper! Come here!" PJ says, with more aggression than I care for. "Down!"

"It's okay—" I begin, but Casper is already trotting to PJ's side.

"She shouldn't be doing that. She's a working dog, but I give her too much leeway."

"Is she ours?" I ask, wondering if I can rescue Casper. I have a brief fantasy of roaming the hills with the collie at my side, but it's immediately punctured by Richard.

"It's PJ's. He runs sheep," Richard explains. "PJ has his own ranch on the eastern border of the estate."

"No money in it," PJ says, spitting into the grass.

"So why do you do it?"

PJ looks at me like I'm an idiot, then gets back in the truck and whistles. Casper jumps into the bed.

As PJ drives off, I turn to Richard, bewildered. "What did I say?"

Richard shakes his head and begins walking to the house. "He's just sentimental. His family used to own this whole place, but his father lost it gambling with commodity futures in the early 1980s. My grandad bought it and turned it into a working cattle ranch. But PJ keeps running sheep like the old days."

I ignore the vibration of my phone coming from my pocket. "Poor guy."

"Don't feel too bad for him. He's sitting on a multi-million-dollar property. He lives like a pauper out of choice. But some people are like that, I guess." He suddenly turns and pulls me into a hug. "By the way, thank you for coming here with me."

It's Richard's first real sign of affection in over a month, and I make the most of it. I quickly wrap my arms around his neck and kiss him, trying my best to feel the spark of affection or desire or *something*. It's not there, but I'm a better actress than I think because I can feel his body responding. Maybe tonight we can end our dry spell.

Around the edges of the house are a few empty flowerbeds and some outdoor furniture, but it all looks cheap and temporary compared to the mansion on the hill above us. A hundred feet away, near the gates, there's an elaborate garden set out in rows, just like an English country estate.

I look across to the mansion and see scaffolding around the entire structure. From the top level, a lean young man in jeans and work boots is staring back at us.

"They won't be here long," Richard says. "Two months, max. They want to be finished before the snow gets too heavy."

"I can't wait," I say, and I mean it. I'm seriously ready to build a new life with my husband in this place.

I glance at the open garage and see a brand-new pickup truck next to a line of boxes from our Manhattan apartment. This is real, I think. We've moved our entire lives to Montana.

"Where's my car?"

"Hasn't arrived yet—it's on order." He unlocks the door and then freezes. "Damn it."

As I walk past him, I immediately start to cough. The air is thick with the stench of marijuana, just about the last smell I'd expect in a house owned by Richard.

I hear a television playing. I follow the sound to the living room, where I find a blonde teenager in black sweatpants stretched out on the couch. While I search for words, she glares at me through bloodshot eyes.

"Who the hell are you? And what are you doing in my house?"

3

JAMES

12 October

I've only been here a day, and I already want to kill him. It's nighttime, and I'm writing this on my mattress on the floor by the light of a single naked bulb. Next to me is my pack. It looks like a wound bleeding out a pile of clothes and some textbooks, which is just about all I brought with me from my old life.

"We'll teach you what we can," the foreman Robert had said. "But you need to keep the floors clean and do what we say."

It was a lie—he has no intention of teaching me anything. I had turned up to the mansion asking for an apprenticeship, but the old man clearly saw me as cheap labor. Robert and Klaus, his German sidekick, look like they're in their fifties, and they're constantly barking at me to do anything heavy or dangerous.

"James! Take this to the dumpster."

"James! Move this door."

More often, they just want me to sweep. Both Robert and Klaus wish to work in pristine conditions.

"James! Floors."

By the end of the day, my arms were exhausted from swinging sledgehammers and carrying timber to the trash. Even sweeping the floors was painful. Writing this now, I feel pain shooting up my arm, the grip of the pen almost too much for my exhausted hand.

But it's not the work I mind; it's how I'm treated. I've never been yelled at more, not even at school. I'm unskilled labor, the bottom of the heap, with less dignity than the collie I see sprinting across the grass at lunchtime. They treat me like a machine that won't do what is written on the box.

I'm getting ahead of myself. Let's go back to the beginning.

I came to this ridiculous place at six, riding my 500cc Suzuki around the turning circle and parking near the front door. As I hopped from foot to foot and rubbed my frozen hands, I stared up at the dark mansion—four stories high and wooden, totally unlike the McMansions I'd driven past on the way here.

Whoever built this place wanted to tell everyone in town one thing: We're better than you.

I looked down to the guest house near the driveway entrance. A light was coming from one of the rooms, and I found myself staring at it, trying to make out a human form through the window.

When the foreman, Robert, arrived an hour later, the sun was up. He looked me up and down and nodded.

"Worked on a building site before?"

I nodded, remembering the lie I had told on the phone. "In the summers."

"You don't look it," he grumbled, walking past me.

I felt like giving him the finger and walking away right then. Even now, I want to take this pen and ram it through his eye socket. But I needed the job, so I followed him into the mansion. He gave me a tour, pointing out the work that needed to be done—the walls that still needed to be finished, others that needed to be ripped out. It looked a long way from finished, but Robert said they'd already been working for six months and had a hard deadline of Christmas.

"Your work will be as boring as hell," he said when we got to the dining room on the second floor. The walls had been opened, the guts of old insulation spilling out. "No apologies about that. We've already been through two apprentices, and I don't want to be stuck without anyone in the last month. Are you sure you're up for it? Speak now or forever hold your peace."

He was staring at my shoulders, just off my eyeline. I could already tell he didn't think I could do it.

"Yep." I went up to the window and looked down at the guest house. "Who lives down there?"

"The Eastwoods. They own the place. They're staying there while we finish up. You might see them come through."

"A family?"

He shakes his head. "Just a couple. Richard Eastman's dad built this place. They're fixing it up before they move in."

I almost laughed. Two people in all this space—it was

absurd. They'd need a dozen kids to fill all the rooms and a full-time staff to keep it clean.

The tour ended in a small, dark room on the ground floor facing the hill. There was a single mattress on the floor and a small fan heater in the corner. It smelled of sawdust.

"This is your quarters." Because of the insane cost of accommodation in Frostwood—a resort town for the nearby glaciers and ski fields—they're giving me a room as part of my contract. "I see you brought your sleeping bag—good. It gets cold at night, but don't run the heater too much. And don't go exploring the estate after work. If you get claustrophobic, go into Frostwood. Keep your distance from the Eastmans. They don't want to see some punk walking around their property at night."

I must have grunted in reply because he prodded me on the back. I swear I almost turned around and smacked him.

"I mean it, kid. You're paid help. They don't want to see you having a beer outside or hear you playing music at night. If you want the room, keep a low profile. And no drugs."

"Sure. Of course."

He thought I was just another barely literate white trash from rural Montana, another young body to chew up before I knocked up some girl or got addicted to meth. What would he say if I told him the truth? That I was summa cum laude, with a full ride to a college out east?

He'd think I was insane to spend my time here, sweeping the floor of a rich man's house. Learning nothing.

But this is what I have to do.

After work, I sat on the grass outside the mansion and enjoyed the late afternoon sun on my face, the fresh air, the view down to Frostwood—anything but the dark, sawdust-filled house I'd been working in all day.

"Be inside by 6 p.m.," Robert yelled as he left the house. That's when Mr. Eastwood would be home. I didn't respond, and he swore to himself before getting in his truck.

I watched him drive down the long gravel drive, past the tiny house to the street, then stood and looked behind me to the north. The property stretched for miles. Maybe if I still needed to be here after Christmas, I could get a job with the rancher who ran it all.

I saw movement by the edge of the forest—a deer. It peered cautiously out, then froze before taking a few more steps. I closed one eye and imagined that I had it in my scope. It was a beautiful doe with light brown coloring—just like one I had seen shot last May by one of my high school friends.

I felt like killing him at the time, a serious, terrifying urge to turn my rifle onto his moronic face. But I'll never see him again. This is the first day of my new life.

The deer startled, then sprinted thirty feet across the forest's edge before disappearing into the trees. Further down, I saw why it bolted—a woman with dark hair wearing skintight black running pants and a sweater. I wondered if she'd followed a trail through the forest and accidentally ended up on private property.

"Don't stare too hard, champ." I jumped at the gruff accented voice of Klaus. "That's the owner's wife."

"I wasn't..." I began, startled. This was Mrs. Eastman? She looked much different than I had imagined—more beautiful but also more normal. I had expected the owner of a place like this never to leave her house without a pearl necklace.

"It's okay. But she's different. That's what you learn working in places like this. These people are practically another species. Want my advice?" He kept talking before I could tell him that, no, I didn't want his damn advice. "Go find a girl in town. Keep you occupied. If you spend all your time in this place, you'll lose your mind."

I kept looking at Mrs. Eastman, and Klaus grunted in annoyance before shuffling off to his van.

He says she's a different breed. Okay—but so am I.

I already know that I'm going to have her.

4

VIRGINIA

"It isn't your house," Richard says from behind me. He's perfectly calm despite the contact high we're all getting just from being in the same room as this girl.

"Our house. Sorry, bro."

Bro? While we both stand there, the girl stares at her phone. A TV plays reruns of the dating show *Too Hot to Handle*.

"Who is this?" I try to keep my voice calm, though part of me wants to snatch the phone from her hand and send it flying through the window.

Richard rubs his temples as if he's suddenly suffering from a powerful migraine. "This is my sister Gillian. I was worried she might turn up."

I glance at the girl and try to do the math. Richard's dad died when Richard was eighteen, and this girl looks like a teenager. She looks young enough to be Richard's daughter.

"I'm right here," Gillian says.

"I'm very much aware of that," Richard replies. "Why are you here, though?"

"The bank took Mom's house after she died. Where else was I meant to go? The old dude let me in." She looks away from her phone and glances at me. "Who's the chick?"

"My wife," Richard replies, calm as ever despite her tone. Sometimes, I wish Richard was the type of man to defend my honor, but that's never been his style. "Are you staying long?"

"Just until I get on my feet. By the way, the cat clock is yours." She points at the wall, where a black cat's curling tail sways back and forth with every tick. "Don't worry, I took some keepsakes as well."

Richard stares at her for a moment, nods briefly, and mutters something about calling the co-working place in town so he can start in the morning. As he leaves the room, the girl looks at me, amused.

"I guess he's not exactly showing off about me at your New York City parties."

"Not exactly," I say like a moron. Gillian still hasn't moved from the couch, so I walk up and hold out my hand. She stares at it for a moment, then takes it.

"Welcome to the family, lady."

Before I can reply, she unmutes the television, and I'm bombarded by the confessions of some half-naked reality TV contestant.

"I'm sorry about your mom," I mutter, taking out my phone. "I'm just going to explore the house."

"Fascinating," Gillian shoots back, and I catch an eye roll before I leave the room.

The house is smaller than Richard's Manhattan apartment. There's a short hallway running down the middle, connecting to three bedrooms and a bathroom. I go into the first bedroom, where Richard has dropped his bag, and find that I still can hear the rumblings of the TV through the wall.

I open the closet. The movers have unpacked my clothes but have left the two boxes labeled 'personal' untouched in the corner. I open the top one and remove the first book, *The Selected Works of John Keats*.

"When I have fears that I may cease to be…"

I immediately close it. I don't know why I kept these books. I studied them at college and then spent the rest of my twenties hauling them around. They're reminders of the type of person I want to be—intelligent, literary, passionate —rather than the person I am. I'm already older than Shelly and Keats when they died. What have I achieved, aside from a pile of debt, a worthless degree, and a marriage on the rocks?

My phone vibrates. I read the message a few times, then quickly scribble a response.

> Leave me alone!

He has my number. Mom must have given it to him. She's the only person on the planet who thinks my ex Steve is a better match for me than Richard.

I place my phone on silent and walk into the bedroom at the end of the hall. This is meant to be the master bedroom, but judging from the mess on the floor, Gillian has already claimed it. Richard's standing beside her bed, looking perplexed.

"Did you sort out the co-working space?"

"Huh?" His expression transforms back to his usual calm self. "Yeah. All sorted."

I wait for him to say something about Gillian. I'm

worried that if I bring it up, I'll sound like I'm complaining. But as he moves towards the door, I can't help myself.

"You have a sister?" I venture.

"Half-sister. That's the first time we've ever met. She's Mom's daughter."

"Really?" I say, trying to keep the surprise from my voice. "It seemed like you knew each other."

"Just on the phone after Mom died."

"It must be nice to see her."

I'm waiting for some explanation of why he's being so passive with this girl. His mother recently died of lung cancer after decades of addiction, and his only other living relative is hotboxing our house. Richard must sense this because he pauses at the door.

"I'm sorry. I know it's not what you were expecting. But her mother just died, you know? I'm the only family she has."

So why didn't you hug her? I wonder. *Why aren't you in there, talking to her?*

Sometimes, I wonder if Richard is dead inside. The only time he says he loves me is during sex, and that's becoming a rare experience. We both need to change—but how?

"Of course," I mutter. "She needs our help."

As he leaves the room, I feel the chances of recapturing the magic—such as it ever was—slipping away.

5

VIRGINIA

It could end tomorrow.

I stop slicing lettuce and look out of the kitchen window at Richard, climbing the hill to the mansion. PJ is walking a few feet behind, with Casper trotting obediently at his side. I wanted to follow him, but he said he needed to talk business with the contractors.

"I can stay," he offered, knowing my response.

"No, go. I'll cook."

What does it take to end a marriage? It should be explosive. Raging arguments and wild insults. There needs to be an affair or a betrayal of some kind. After all, a marriage seems like such a solid thing. There are documents to sign and government entities to inform. People say vows to each other, to the state, to God. They change their entire identities.

But then you're in it, and you realize it's still just two people that share a feeling. A feeling! Nothing more substantial than air trapped in a balloon. If you loosen your grip for too long, it can just *disappear*.

In a moment, your entire life can end.

"I can see why he married you." I turn to see Gillian standing in the doorway, staring at my body. "How many hours in the gym did that take? Or did you skip all that and just get a BBL?"

It takes me a second to process what she said. "What's that?"

"Look it up." She licks her lips, then cackles. "Honestly, you're an inspiration. If I just spend years in the gym and suppress my entire personality, I might land a rich dude and never work another day in my life. I'll get to spend my life in the kitchen or..." She pauses. "On my back?"

I'm so confused by her hostility that I can't speak.

"There's that famous wit." She raises a mock gun to her head and pulls the trigger. "He didn't even tell you about me, did he? I thought marriage was supposed to be about open communication, but I guess the rules are different for guys as rich as my brother. He didn't marry you for conversation, did he? Better find a gym in town, or he'll be on the lookout for a younger model."

"It's not like that," I say weakly as she grabs an apple from the fruit bowl.

"Sure, darling." She rolls her eyes and then walks back to the living room.

I look down at the lettuce and am mortified to find tears in my eyes. Somehow, this kid has nailed all of my deepest fears. Because it's true. Sometimes I feel like I'm not a wife but a junior employee at a corporation, praying that my boss doesn't realize what a terrible job I'm doing.

I've always been afraid to push Richard too hard in case he realizes that I'm not the effortlessly beautiful, softly spoken English major he fell in love with.

It's pathetic, I know. But I can't afford for him to leave me. Not yet.

I drop the knife and check my phone. There are a few more messages. I delete them all without reading them, then scrawl a message to Mom.

> Please tell me you didn't give Steve my new number?!

I spend the next hour making chicken salad, which Richard and I share at the small kitchen table. We talk about the logistics of the move and exchange cliches about how excited we are to live in this beautiful place.

"You can teach me how to ski," I say. "And ride horses."

"I'll have to learn first."

There it is again. I'm always forgetting where he came from. Even though he's wealthy now, he didn't grow up with a silver spoon in his mouth. I love that about him—those rough edges, that sense of the iceberg lurking under his calm exterior.

But if he's an iceberg, then what am I? The Titanic?

I make a plate for Gillian and place it on the coffee table. She gives a dismissive snort without looking up from her phone, but I know that when I come back later, it'll all be gone. I wonder how long it's been since she ate a proper meal. She looks pale, almost skeletal, and I can't help but feel sorry for her. She's a wildcat, but she's just lost her mother, and Richard isn't exactly giving her a warm welcome. I want to pull her into a hug and tell her it'll all get better with time.

She'd probably punch me in the mouth if I tried. Besides, what do I know? Who says it all gets better, anyway?

"How was the big house?" I say, later, as I pull off my tights. I'm tired from the day, but my legs are still jumpy.

"Fine." He gets changed with his back to me, facing the window.

"Sort out the contractors?"

He sits down on the bed. It's been a while since I've slept on a cheap mattress, and I have to stop myself rolling in his direction.

"What?"

"The contractors," I say as he rubs his eyes. "Did you sort them out?"

"Oh, yeah. It's all good up there. They'll be done in six weeks."

"Damn."

He turns to me, frowning. "It's a big job. They've already been going for months. Surely it's not the end of the world—"

"Hey, hey," I say, raising my hands. "I wasn't saying anything. I don't mind it here. Even with—"

"Gillian's been through a lot," he snaps. "Come on, I'm expecting us to make an effort."

"I know." I reach across and touch his shoulder. "It's okay. I know you're stressed from the move."

He touches my hand briefly, then stands up to switch off the light. I see him about to put his earplugs in, so I pull the comforter across and pat the bed.

"What are you doing?" he asks.

I can't believe it. I'm lying in my underwear on the bed, and he's asking what I'm doing. I've never had to try this hard to sleep with a man. "What do you think? Let's christen the house."

"Aren't you exhausted?" he says. There's a joking lilt to his voice, but I can tell he's trying to put me off.

"Not yet."

He leans towards me, and I think this is going to be it: A new beginning. But then he turns away from my kiss and pecks me on the cheek.

"Another time."

As he switches off the light and turns his back to me, I feel them again, those pesky tears. I immediately blink them away.

I want to punch him. I want to make him understand how many men would jump at the chance. I want to threaten to leave.

But instead, I quietly put on my pajamas and close my eyes. I try to tell myself that he really is just exhausted.

And I push away the nagging, far-too-logical question: Has he really been exhausted for three months straight?

6

VIRGINIA

When I wake the following day, I feel groggy, almost like I've been drugged. I must have been more tired than I thought.

I feel the bounce of the bed and crack my eyes open.

"What's going on?" He's sitting on the bed, buttoning a white shirt. It's a familiar scene ever since I quit my job in New York and moved into his fancy apartment—him dressing in a suit while I laze around in bed.

"What do you think? It's a weekday, Virginia."

"It's our first day." I can't keep the disbelief from my voice. We've moved our lives across the country, and he's taken precisely one day off work.

"It's at a critical stage," he says, leaning across and giving me a peck on the cheek. I don't bother asking what he's talking about. It's been years since I had anything to do with GSP Engineering, and I was never at his level.

"When can you take some time off?"

"Huh?" He's searching through the ties that are lined up in the wardrobe. "Christmas."

I turn away from him, holding in my anger. I can't complain. I knew this was what it would be like when we got married. But is it crazy to hope that we'd be able to explore the area together on our first day?

"I don't even have a car."

"Virginia, I'm late." He goes to the mirror and adjusts his tie. He looks immaculate—though I'm not sure why he needs to wear a suit just to sit on video calls all day. "We're living on a massive ranch. Go exploring."

I close my eyes, holding back the rebuttals that creep into my mind. Somehow, every conversation we have turns into an argument.

Still, I wonder. Why did he have a car waiting for him, and I didn't?

"I'll be home by six. Just got some calls with Asia."

I force a smile as he bends down for his trademark peck. But as soon as I hear the front door close, I yell into my pillow. I've moved to Montana to give us a fresh start on our marriage. But how's that going to happen if he's never around?

I fumble for my phone and see that I've got a reply from Mom.

> He just got out, sweetie. I didn't see the harm.

That was the problem with Mom—she never saw the harm, even when it was right in front of her face. She didn't see the harm in my dad, who terrorized her until he finally dropped dead from a heart attack. She didn't see the harm in the revolving door of alcoholics and deadbeats that shared her bed throughout the rest of my childhood.

You're ruining my life!

I type, then delete the message. I sound like a child; besides, arguing with my mom is never a great idea. She's famously stubborn and never backs down from a fight. That's one reason why the men in her life never stay more than a few months.

Besides, it isn't true. Steve has my number, but he doesn't know where I am. If I were in New York, I'd be constantly looking over my shoulder.

But out in Montana, I can be free.

I tiptoe past Gillian's closed door and make a coffee with my bright red La Marzocco Linea Mini espresso machine. It had been a birthday present from Richard and was precisely twice as expensive as the 1992 Mazda I drove before we met.

While my beans grind, I clean up Richard's dishes. He makes his favorite breakfast of eggs on toast—sunny side up —every day, though he still hasn't figured out how to put his plate in the dishwasher.

Is this my life? Kissing my husband before work, doing his dishes, and preparing his meals?

I shake my head and force a smile. Gillian is already in my head, but she's wrong. I didn't come to Montana to be a maid. As Richard and I agreed before we moved, I came for another reason entirely. Something that will make our bond permanent, whether we love each other or not.

I came to be a mother.

As the beans finish grinding, I smile for real. Soon, I'll live in a mansion on the hill with a house full of children. And who knows? Maybe I'll be able to start writing again.

I watch with satisfaction as the shot of espresso dribbles into the cup, then steam my almond milk. With the foam, I make a pattern of a question mark. I'm so close to a real life I can almost taste it.

I take my coffee outside and sit on the porch, overlooking the extensive gardens. A Hispanic woman is bent over a line of rose bushes, pulling out weeds. I imagine all the other staff I will have one day. A cleaner to scrub Richard's dishes. A private chef. Maybe even a nanny.

I take a sip of coffee—then spit it out. It tastes bitter, almost like it's been brewed with seawater. I toss it onto the grass and then return inside. I test the filter, but the water's fine, and the beans smell fresh. I take off the grinder and tip the leftover coffee onto the bench, and that's when I see the culprit.

A sprinkle of white within the dark grounds. Salt! Someone's put salt into my coffee grinder.

And I immediately know who that someone is.

7

VIRGINIA

As I run water through the machine, I tell myself it's a prank. She's hostile, true—but maybe that's just her way of testing the limits of... what? An authority figure? Is that what I am? It's a crazy assumption because I've never had power over anyone in my entire life. I've only ever been on the lowest rung of the ladder.

A daughter, a student, an employee.

Maybe she's worried that I'll try to parent her. But honestly, that's the last thing I want to do. She's eighteen, which is an adult in my books. She's free to make her own mistakes and deal with the consequences.

God knows I did at her age.

It would be nice to have a sister, but for now, I'll accept the awkward, polite, small talk of a houseguest.

I take my second coffee outside and look at the garden. It's mostly past its peak bloom. The paths between the flowerbeds are littered with dead leaves.

A cemetery of petals, I say to myself—the season's graveyard.

I think about getting a pad and scribbling some lines, but I know that the words will stop as soon as I make it real. I can only write in my head.

What does that make my brain? A mausoleum of poetry?

Enough! Unlike the dead petals and leaves of the garden, these lines don't compost into new life. They're more like radioactive waste, a poisonous reminder of who I once wanted to be. A poet! What an insane ambition. I want to curse Mom and all those teachers for encouraging me, but I know I'm to blame.

I need to accept who I am. A wife. A mother, soon. That's enough for anyone.

"It's beautiful, isn't it?"

The gardener looks up at me, frowns, then returns to her work. Maybe she doesn't speak English? I walk closer and see she's adding mulch, presumably to help the plants get through the winter.

I decide to have another go. I don't want to be one of those rich people who ignores the help, especially when I still feel like I *am* the help.

"Where are you from?"

She glances up at me and speaks with that Montana twang. "Seriously?"

"Sorry, I just thought..." I feel mortified. I can almost guess her next question—would you ask that about any of the white people around here?

I silently pray that this woman will give me the benefit of the doubt—the first person to do so in this godforsaken state —but I can already see that my prayer won't be answered.

She stands up slowly, cracks her knuckles like she's preparing for a fight, and then swings the sack of dead leaves over her shoulders. "I'm from right here."

"Here?" I manage, weakly.

"I'm Native," she says. "This was our land. For thousands of years."

My mouth hangs open, and I pray that something intelligent will tumble out. But for the second time that morning, my prayers are ignored.

"Oh. Wow."

She gives me a withering look, and I feel the heat of a blush around my neck. Why is everything so hard? I've made a faux pas, but does she have to be rude about it?

"I've got work to do," she says, walking past me. When the sack of leaves scrapes against my shoulder, I tell myself it's an accident.

Because what else could it be?

8

VIRGINIA

After my coffee, I change into my running clothes and set off to explore the property. I run north until I hit a waist-high fence, and continue alongside it until I see a gate shut by a bolt running through a thick chain. Once I'm through the fence, I keep going along a heavily potholed four-wheel-drive track dotted with dark mounds of cow shit.

Half a mile further, I see three enormous cows blocking my way. The closest one stares at me but doesn't move. I have a vague sense that it should be scared of me, but as I get closer, it continues to stare. I know it can't hurt me, but something about its size and serenity makes me want to sprint in the other direction.

"It's okay, girls," I say ridiculously as I inch around the cattle. "I'm a friend."

Once I'm past them, I keep running for a few minutes until I hit another fence—this one almost up to my shoulders. On the other side, half a dozen horses are staring into the distance or idly chewing grass.

"Hey there," I say to the closest horse, and to my surprise, it ambles in my direction. I stare up at it, astonished by its beauty. "What's your name?"

I look beyond the horse, and I'm immediately struck by the proximity of the Rockies. The mountains and glaciers are so immense that they are difficult to take in. What did the poets call this, this mixture of terror and beauty? Sublime.

But then, what did they know? They were writing about ponds and hills compared to this. We need new words for this immense landscape, a new language.

"Hey! Don't do that!"

I turn to find PJ striding towards me from my right on the other side of the fence. There's an ATV beside him. He must have been watching me the entire time.

"What's wrong?" I say.

"He's a biter." He immediately rubs the horse's flank as if to show how little affinity I have with these animals. "You know anything about horses?"

It's an innocent question, but with his tone, it feels like an accusation.

"Not much."

He grunts, then looks back in the direction of the ATV. "Keep your distance around these animals until you know what you're doing. Even those cows will give you a nasty kick if you get too close."

How do you know I got close to the cows? I think to myself. I have the strange sense that this man has been watching me this entire time, even though I know that can't be true. I would have heard the engine of his ATV.

"PJ," I say as he walks off. I make my voice an octave

lower and hope it makes me sound more authoritative than I feel.

He raises his eyebrows by way of a response.

"Who is the gardener? She wouldn't tell me her name."

He looks in the general direction of the house and smiles faintly as if a joke was painted across the landscape. "That's Simone. She's worked in the gardens there for years."

"And where does this path go?"

"It's not safe to just walk around the ranch alone," he says, ignoring my question. "There's a trail into the forest a few hundred feet back the way you came. Get your exercise there."

It sounds like an order. Before I can think of something else to say, he's striding back to his ATV. And even though I hate myself, I run towards the trailhead. He's right—I have no business being on this ranch.

But I'm going to learn. I'll have to if I'm going to make my life here.

9

VIRGINIA

I spend the afternoon preparing a roast chicken for dinner, something I used to do when Richard and I first moved in together. I drizzle garlic butter across the surface of the chicken, then use a length of string to tie up the drumsticks. When the oven is hot, I put it in and set a timer on my watch for seventy-five minutes.

"Smells good," Gillian says.

"Uh, thanks," I say, waiting for the insult to land. But she just grabs a lemonade from the fridge and flashes me a smile.

"Can't wait to try it?" she asks with an expectant, vulnerable lilt.

"Uh... of course."

"Awesome. Thanks, Virginia."

It takes me a minute to recover from Gillian's bizarre onslaught of kindness. I wonder for a second if maybe she hadn't poured salt into my coffee machine. Maybe it got there accidentally? Or one of the movers had done it?

I spend the next hour taking a bath. I shave my legs, then

wash and condition my hair. None of it needs doing—at least, not to the standards I'd kept in New York—but I have to keep trying. Richard can be an asshole, but that's mostly because he works too hard. I still love him, and he's still going to be the father of my children.

I'm in my towel when the timer goes off. Despite the season, I slip into a billowy sundress that Richard likes and rush out to finish dinner.

I spend the next few minutes finishing the potatoes and salad and carefully plating the food. I give us both the drumsticks and leave Gillian to carve what she wants. By the time I finish, it's just past six. I pour us both a wine, then go to the living room.

"Do you want to eat with us?" I ask Gillian. She's staring at her phone, apparently confused at something on her screen.

"I'll have some later." She pauses and then smiles sweetly. "Thanks, Virginia."

I'm stunned, and when Richard comes home a minute later, I still have a grin plastered across my face.

"Someone had a good day?" he says, kissing me on the cheek.

"I... don't know," I say. "I met some cows. And a horse. And got told off by PJ. I even met our gardener."

"You're keeping busy," he says, though I can tell he's not listening. "What's this?"

It sounds almost like an accusation, but I try to ignore it. "Dinner," I say, putting my arm around his waist. "It isn't much..."

"You're a gem." He sits at the table, sniffs the wine, then pops a fried potato in his mouth. "Delicious."

"Don't get used to it, buddy," I joke. "Special occasions only."

He glances at me and grins. For a second, I see something familiar I thought I'd lost over the last year—something like the calm and playful man I fell in love with.

I watch him slice through the chicken, then gasp at what I see.

"Jesus!" He pushes the plate away like it's radioactive. The drumstick is still pink and bloody. "How long did you cook this for?"

"The normal time," I say. "I don't know how this happened..."

"You know how busy I am at work. I can't get sick, Virginia. Especially not from something as downright idiotic as food poisoning."

I feel myself blushing. How did it happen? The oven was hot when I put the chicken in, and it had stayed that way the whole time. Hadn't it?

The only way this chicken could still be raw is if the oven was faulty.

"What's going on?" Gillian asks from the doorway, before making a retching sound. "Uh, let me cancel my order."

As she leaves, I realize that there's a second possibility. Someone could have turned the oven off when I went to my bath and switched it back on just before I got out.

"It's okay," Richard says, sighing heavily. "I'll fill up on potatoes and a protein shake."

"That's no dinner," I say.

"It's fine."

I watch as he blends the shake, then silently wolfs down his potatoes. A normal wife would ask questions about his day, and a normal husband would try to find something interesting to respond. But we aren't normal anymore.

Still, I'm not about to give up. While Richard's in the shower, I change into something lacy that I haven't had the confidence to wear in months. I stand in front of the mirror and convince myself I'm still attractive. Tonight could be the night.

I lie in bed nervously while I listen to him brushing his teeth. When he comes out, he's already in his pajamas. And when he looks at me, I know he isn't in the mood. Until I married Richard, I didn't realize that was something that actually existed. In my dating life before him, men always wanted to have as much sex as possible. The only move I ever needed was to say yes.

But before Richard, I'd never slept with someone older than thirty. Maybe this is just what older men are like?

I stand up and walk over to him. Before he can say no, I kiss him and reach down to his pajamas.

"Virginia," he says, taking my hand.

"Yes?" I whisper as seductively as I can manage.

"Not tonight." He kisses me back, a chaste, familial kiss. "I'm sorry."

"It's not your fault," I say, trying to blink away the tears. I give him an excuse to save me the humiliation. "You're tired."

"I'm an old man." He flops onto the bed and reaches for his phone.

"You're not even forty," I shoot back.

"Huh?" he says, already scrolling through something—probably baseball scores.

I try to swallow my anger, but it's too much. We've come all this way, and he isn't even trying.

"Forget it."

As I march half-naked toward the bathroom, I hear a wolf whistle coming from Gillian's room, followed by a laugh. I slam the bathroom door, then squeeze my hands into fists. When I loosen them again, I see that the nail on my ring finger has broken through the skin on my left hand.

I let the blood fall into the sink and wonder, how far can one person be pushed before she snaps, once and for all?

10

JAMES

14 October

I was sweeping the enormous living room on the second floor when I heard a terrible sound. Deep, gruff, authoritative.

Mr. Eastman.

His voice came from just down the hall, interspersed with the foreman, Robert. I froze, unsure of where to go. The voices disappeared for a moment. I figured he'd taken Mr. Eastman into the dining room, so I darted into the hallway and sprinted downstairs. I locked myself in the toilet until he was gone.

Now that I see it written down, it sounds childish. But I don't want to see him until I have to. I don't want to like or hate him; I honestly don't want to risk thinking of him as a human being.

After all, it might make it more difficult to seduce his wife.

That was this morning, the fourth morning of my stay at

the Eastman Estate. Everything hurt. I needed to rest my sore muscles and let the blisters heal on my hands and toes, but Robert and Klaus didn't give me a moment to myself. They were always hovering, waiting for one job to finish before sending me to the next.

I'm allowed ten minutes off in the morning and thirty minutes for lunch. The only good part is that we start early, meaning I can finish at four and wait for her outside. She runs or hikes in the forest every afternoon, and I always make sure that I watch her—though I first wait for Klaus to leave. I don't want to risk him getting the wrong idea.

The wrong idea being the truth—that I want her.

I need to cool it. I can't stop thinking about her, but this horny desperation isn't going to get me anywhere. I wonder if I should go into Frostwood and find a lonely tourist to take the edge off, but I already know it won't help.

After Mr. Eastman left, I spent the rest of the day in a funk. I could tell that Robert and Klaus were impressed by the man, as they worked me harder than ever. As I went from painfully carrying timber upstairs to painfully sweeping the floor, I knew I couldn't wait much longer. I had to make progress. Another week of being yelled at by Klaus, and I'd punch him—or, worse, come to accept it as normal.

I needed a miracle. And a few minutes before knockoff, I got it. I was leaning on my broom in one of the upstairs bedrooms, pretending to sweep, when I heard the voice.

Her voice. Mrs. Eastman.

They moved quickly down the hall, and before I could think, she was standing only a few feet away from me. She was wearing tight blue jeans and a woolen coat—a beautiful, expensive anomaly next to Robert, who looks like he's been bathing in sawdust for decades.

"Miss, this is James. The apprentice."

She smiled at me and extended her arm.

"Hi," I said, raising my hands. "I won't touch you if that's okay."

"What's wrong with your hands?"

I showed her my palms. They were covered in blisters, some popped and raw.

"He's green," Robert said, rolling his eyes. "They'll callous in no time."

"Do you have a first-aid kit?"

"Ma'am, with respect—" Robert began, but Mrs. Eastman interrupted.

"You know it's illegal to force a man to work without proper first aid? He's bleeding, for crying out loud."

"This is a building site."

"And he's a person. And this is America. He has rights!"

Robert stared at Mrs. Eastman momentarily before muttering under his breath and leaving the room. When he was gone, she took my hand and looked at my blisters. I felt a charge of electricity rush through my body. It felt like I was in seventh grade again and holding hands was the biggest thrill in the world. I could have stood like that forever, but to my horror, my hand was beginning to shake. I had thought about this moment for too long; it was making me nervous.

I couldn't have her think I was just a terrified boy, so I pulled my hand away.

"You didn't need to do that. It's fine."

She looked up at me, smirking. "Oh, I know. I just don't like being treated like a dumb little woman."

"You used me."

"My motives were noble."

"No, they weren't."

At this, she burst out laughing. "I suppose not." She walked to the window and looked out at the view. I regretted that she wasn't close to me anymore, that she wasn't still touching me. "It feels nice to have power over someone. I'm still not used to being in that position. I'm usually the one getting ordered around."

"Story of my life."

"Story of everyone's lives."

As I watched her, I had doubts about my plan. How would I, a boy who grew up with food stamps and an addict for a mother, ever hope to attract a woman like that? It's true that girls notice me—they always have, ever since puberty. At first, they talked about my green eyes; then, when I started working out, it was my arms and abs. Girls were simple like that.

But this wasn't a girl. She was a sophisticated woman with a millionaire husband.

"No," I ventured. "It isn't."

She laughed again. "That's the second time you've corrected me."

"With respect, that's the second time you've been wrong."

She was about to respond when Robert returned with a metal box. He opened it on the floor and fumbled around for a plaster.

"Let me," Mrs. Eastman said, snatching the plaster from Robert. Without asking, she grabbed my hand and randomly stuck the plaster down. When I looked at her, she winked. "There. All better."

"Thank you," I muttered.

Robert coughed. "Maybe we should keep moving. It's been a long day, miss, and we're about to finish up."

"I don't mind," I said.

"What?" Robert asked. I saw Mrs. Eastman grinning behind him.

"I can take her on the tour. If you need to get home."

"I've got it, James."

I decided not to object. The last thing I needed was for Robert to guess my intentions. As she passed by me to leave the room, I noticed that she was carrying a book of poems by William Wordsworth. I touched her on the elbow.

"I love that book," I said, keeping my voice low so Robert couldn't hear, before quoting a line from a poem I memorized in high school. "We have given away our hearts."

She gave me a surprised smile. I recognized it at once—I've been getting it from teachers my entire life. No one ever expects a guy like me to be anything but an idiot, let alone quote poetry from memory.

"For this, for everything, we are out of tune," she said. "I know what Wordsworth means. Look at this monstrosity. People think this building is beautiful, but I think they've lost their minds."

"Miss!" Robert called from down the hall.

"I'd rather be a pagan," I said, quoting a line from the end of the poem. She frowned this time, just slightly, and then rushed to catch up with Robert.

11

VIRGINIA

I wake at six on our first Saturday in Montana to find Richard packing by the light of his phone. Half-asleep, I wonder if he's leaving me. But then I see his rifle leaning against the foot of the bed.

"You're going hunting?" I croak.

"The season's almost over." He leans over and kisses me. "I'm sorry. I know it's bad timing. But the snow's coming in soon."

"It's our first weekend!"

"I know. But there'll be plenty more."

He zips up his pack and slings it over his shoulder. In the dim light, I can imagine what he must have looked like as a soldier twenty years earlier. Lean and dark, with a full head of hair and those intense eyes—he would have been irresistible, even without the uniform.

"Come back to bed," I say, smiling. We haven't had sex in the morning since our honeymoon, and even then, it partly felt like an obligation. I try to look as seductive as possible, but Richard pretends not to notice.

"Raincheck. I've got a long drive ahead." He picks up his rifle and then switches off the light on his torch. "Relax. I'll be back on Sunday night. With dinner, hopefully."

Before I can complain, he shuts the door, and I'm alone.

Well, not entirely alone.

A few hours later, I wake to the sound of hip-hop music coming through the wall. Cursing, I sit up and rub the sleep from my eyes before opening the bottom drawer of the nightstand and removing a small metallic box from underneath a pile of books. Inside is a blister pack of pills. I take it, then put the box back beneath the pile.

As I open my door, I'm confronted by a cloud of smoke. In the living room, I see Gillian back on the couch, staring at her phone with a joint in her left hand.

"Can you turn that down?" I yell, coughing loudly.

Gillian doesn't react. I notice that her AirPods are on, so I grab the remote from the coffee table and switch off the music videos playing on the TV.

"Hey!" she complains. "Put that back on!"

"Please, it's early," I say. "And you're not even watching it."

"Are you a mind-reader? I was just checking a text." As she stares at me, she takes a long hit of her joint and exhales the smoke in my direction. "And it's almost lunchtime."

Lunch? I must have slept later than I thought. According to the doctors, I needed to keep my routines as regular as possible. But that will be hard in Montana, where I have no job, no friends, and no hobbies. I don't even have a husband to spend my weekends with.

"Can you please not do this inside?" I ask, waving the smoke away. "Some of us don't want to get a contact high every time we walk in the front door."

"It's cold out," she mutters before putting her AirPods back in.

I stare at her for a moment, unsure of what to do. It's been a while since I interacted with a teenager, and they were mostly interns at work who were dying to impress me. Those kids were ambitious, hyper-organized, do-their-homework-early types.

Gillian was another breed. From the little Richard told me, she was a high school dropout with no skills, job, or plans. Though they had a similar upbringing, they couldn't be more different. Richard, for one, hated drugs. His mother was an addict, so he went in the opposite direction. He didn't even believe in antidepressants. Whereas Gillian looked to be doing her best to follow in her mother's footsteps.

On a whim, I cross the room and push open two windows, letting in a draft of chill October air.

"Bitch!" Gillian says as I leave the room, smiling to myself.

The feeling of satisfaction doesn't last. As I put a load of Richard's shirts into the washing machine, I remind myself that Gillian had just lost her mother to an overdose. I have no idea what it's like to be raised by an addict, but it can't be easy. Richard had the same childhood, but he never talked about it. I know that after graduating high school, he left home and never spoke to his mother again. Once he got the inheritance from his father, he stepped into a new life and pretended his old life never existed.

As far as I know, this is the first time Richard's even stepped foot in Montana in eighteen years.

I step outside with a coffee and check my phone. Another text from Steve. It's my fault for responding. I'm like a fish circling his line, nibbling his bait, giving him hope that I might let myself be reeled in.

> You're not pregnant yet. You don't love him.
> You just want his money.

My hand hovers over my phone's 'block' button, but I don't press it. The only thing worse than getting harassed by Steve is wondering what he's plotting in secret.

> I can still remember you. I can still smell
> you. I know you remember it, too. You said
> it was forever.

When I married Richard, I decided to sever ties with Steve forever. I got a new phone and changed my routine so Steve couldn't track me down when he got out. When Richard suggested we move to Montana, I thought this would be my chance to lose him for good. This is supposed to be our fresh start. Our clean slate.

> If you stay with him, you'll die. He's sucking
> the life out of you, Virginia.

I put my phone away. Steve has the power to destroy me, but he doesn't know it. He thinks Richard knows the truth about my past. But I've kept a secret from my husband—and it needs to stay that way.

"You ready?"

I turn to see Simone standing by the front door. She's wearing knee-high boots and a cowboy hat.

"Hi...?" I manage. "Ready for what?"

"The ride? Richard set it up. He said you needed to learn."

I look across to see two large horses, both with dark coats and white spots.

This is it, I think. *This is what true love feels like.*

"Of course I'm ready."

12

VIRGINIA

An hour later, we're crossing a small creek a few miles to the north. Janet, my horse, is calm and steady and has kept to a slow trot the entire way.

"You sore yet?" Simone calls out.

I think about acting tough but decide there's no point pretending. This is the first time I've ever touched a horse, let alone ridden one.

"It's worth it."

"Talk to me tomorrow and see."

These are the first words she's spoken to me during the entire ride. We went right to the northern edge of the ranch, then continued along a public trail into the foothills. As we cross the creek, the trail narrows to a single-file path, which winds deeper into the hillside.

"Hey, Simone. Can we stop here?"

I pull my foot free of the stirrups and prepare to get off. But to my horror, Simone continues her way along the path. She gives a low whistle without turning around, and Janet trots after her. "Easy, girl," I whisper, clutching her as tightly as I can between my thighs and trying to get my foot back in the stirrup. As I do so, I glance to my left and feel a jolt of panic. There's only a few inches between Janet's hoof and the trail's edge.

"Five more minutes," Simone calls out. "There's a lookout just ahead."

With that, she begins to trot even faster along the narrow path. Janet instinctively follows her pace, and I find it impossible to get my foot back in position with the jolting horse.

"Can we slow down?" I ask, but Simone pretends not to hear me. Clutching the reins as tightly as I can, I try to force my foot back in the stirrups and accidentally kick Janet in the side. She immediately doubles her pace—and I find myself falling. I cling to the reins long enough to free my other foot and leap clear of the panicked horse.

A moment later, I'm lying in the dust, ten feet down from the trail, trying to figure out if any of my bones are broken.

"Virginia! For Christ's sake, what did you do?" Simone scrambles down the bank to meet me. "You could have died. How did it even happen?"

I sit up, sore but relieved that I don't seem seriously injured. Above me, the two horses are looking down at us patiently. "I'm okay."

"I'm glad. But seriously, how did you fall?"

"I told you I wanted to stop! I had a foot out of the stirrup—"

"You what?" Her eyes flash with anger. "I'm responsible for you out here. You can't do things like that without telling me."

I let out a groan as I try to stand up. I'm going to be bruised all over tomorrow. "It's my first time. Why did you insist on going up that path?"

She raises an eyebrow and snorts dismissively. "I took my six-year-old niece up that trail last week. Literally. She thought it was exciting."

I climb awkwardly back up across the rocks to the trail and run my hand across Janet's flank. "I'm sorry about that," I murmur. "It wasn't your fault."

Then, I continue up the path on my own.

"Where are you going?" Simone calls out.

I keep going without answering. Five minutes later, I'm on the lookout—a small tower with an ancient, barely legible map pointing out local landmarks. I sit on a chipped green wooden seat and look out to the town of Frostwood. There are a few more prominent buildings in the center of town, but it looks like a suburb for the most part. The backyards of houses grow in size the further out you get, turning gradually into the lifestyle blocks and farms bordering the Eastwood Estate.

I hear panting behind me, and soon Simone is sitting beside me. She taps my shoulder and hands me a turkey sandwich.

"You're not vegetarian or anything?"

I bite into the sandwich and focus on the scene ahead. Simone is clearly uncomfortable, but I admire her capacity to sit with the awkwardness. We've just yelled at each other, but she's determined—or incapable—of doing anything but pretend it didn't happen.

Maybe one day I'll be like that, I think. Montana-tough. This lonely, taciturn toughness that makes it seem like you hate everything and everyone.

To my horror, I find that there are tears in my eyes. I try to wipe them away before Simone notices, but it's too late.

"Jesus, I thought you weren't hurt."

"Sorry," I mutter. "You weren't supposed to see that."

She's quiet for a minute. "It's just a horse ride. People fall off all the time."

I wait until I'm sure my voice is steady before replying. "It's not that. It's... everything."

"Where are you from? New York?"

"Queens."

She hands me an apple, and I reluctantly take it. I'm starving and know I'll need the energy to get home again.

"I'm just so alone out here," I say.

"It's a bit different, I bet. Not as many creature comforts." I glare at her, but she doesn't notice my reaction. "This is real life. We grow and kill for our food. We're outside every day, rain or shine. If we fall over, we have to get up again, or we don't eat. We don't rely on other people to get by. If someone attacks, we defend ourselves. And we don't cry about it like you folks on the coasts."

I search for a rebuttal against this tide of bullshit. I want to tell her how wrong she is, how much she doesn't understand what's happening in my life.

But before I can respond, she stands and gives me her last piece of unsolicited advice.

"The fact is, you don't belong here," she says. "You're just a tourist, Virginia. It's written all over your face. I know it, PJ knows it, the damn horses know it. Maybe it's time you figured it out for yourself before it's too late. Go back to your own people. You'll save yourself a lot of sadness."

13

VIRGINIA

Richard arrives home after dark the next day. Last night, I planned on telling him everything Simone said to me. I stewed on it for hours. She's our gardener, for Christ's sake. What right did she have to tell me I didn't belong in the state?

But as I went on my run the next day, I began to think she was right. I didn't belong here, and there was a real chance I would be miserable here, living alone. I had fallen off my horse and cried like a child. It was pathetic.

I was pathetic.

"How was the hunt?" I ask.

He keeps his head down and seems intent on setting a new record for demolishing his meal. I've cooked pasta and meatballs—something not even Gillian can cause me to mess up.

"Fine." I can see the familiar shadows under his eyes. He's tired again and doesn't seem any happier.

"Who did you go with?"

"Just some locals."

I carefully twirl a line of pasta around my fork and consciously make my voice soft so he can't take my next comment as an accusation. "How do you know any locals?"

"PJ." He takes a sip of water, then looks at me for the first time that meal. "He said you were up at the house."

I bristle at the realization that PJ has been spying on me. "I had a tour."

"Stay away from there until it's done."

"Is that an order?" I ask. "I was there with the builders. They can tell me if it's unsafe."

"No, they won't. You're my wife. They won't question you."

I pick up his plate and take it to the sink. Mine is only half-eaten, but I don't feel hungry anymore. "It seems like I'm getting nothing but questions ever since I got here."

"What's that supposed to mean, Virginia?"

I can't stand the condescension in his tone, so I shake my head and walk down to our room before I say something I'll regret. There's music coming from the living room, but it's not as bad as it was on Saturday. I open my phone and scroll down my texts till I find my old friends. It's been over a year since I spoke to any of them. After I married Richard, my life was suddenly so much different than theirs.

At the time, I thought my life would get so much better. But instead, I'm just alone.

I think about sending a text to the defunct group chat when I hear Richard let out a cry of anger. I cross my fingers that he's finally speaking his mind to Gillian, but then he yells my name.

"Virginia! What did you do?"

Richard has never been one to yell like that, so I jog

down the hall to the laundry room. He's standing in front of a basket of wet clothes, all dyed a shade of pink.

"Christ, this is a thousand dollars' worth of shirts! Ruined!"

"Oh, no..." I crouch down and sift through the clothes until I find the culprit. A pair of my red underwear. "I don't know how this happened."

"Seems pretty obvious to me."

"No." I ball them up in my hand. "I mean, I haven't even worn these since we arrived!"

He kicks the basket and steps past me into the hall.

"Richard, it was an accident."

"Well, it's an extremely stupid one," he snaps. "What are you even doing washing my shirts? I get them dry cleaned."

"I just thought because we're in the middle of nowhere—"

"Stop being so dramatic! Frostwood is practically a small city, and it's ten miles down the road. Don't you think they have dry cleaners here? Just because it's not New York—"

"How am I supposed to know? I don't even have a car!"

"It's on order, Virginia, as I've told you. More than once. What's going on with you these days?"

There's so much I want to say, but I have enough presence of mind to hold my tongue. Richard is being an ass, but he's right to be angry. His shirts are ruined.

Except it isn't my fault. It's Gillian. She's trying to make us miserable—and maybe even drive us apart.

I have no idea why.

But so far, it's working.

14

JAMES

17 October

A would-be stepfather once said, there is no life without purpose; well, she has become my purpose. I spend my days sweeping and carrying scraps of wood, moving furniture and timber until my muscles ache.

And then, stiff and resentful, I do it all again.

Nothing ever changes. Nothing adds up. Everyone else in the house spends their days making things new again. They work for a day, and a wall is rebuilt, a room re-wired, a kitchen plumbed. There's nothing like that for me. Without her, I'd go mad within a week. I hardly talk to anyone, not even the contractors that come through. At lunchtime, I eat a sandwich on the hill overlooking the house where she lives, trying to get a glimpse of her.

She did not run today. I waited till it was dark and the frost descended, and then I waited some more. As I write this, my hands are still numb from the cold.

I could be at college, getting my degree, sleeping with girls in my dorm, taking my place in the world. God knows I've been waiting for years to escape.

But I can't leave yet.

Not until I'm free.

18 October

I spent the entire day demolishing a wall and carrying the broken timber to the skip. It was almost enjoyable. The blisters on my hands are becoming callouses. The house is slowly transforming. Mrs. Eastman (I realize I don't even know her first name) said that the house was ugly, but I think she's wrong. It's out of place, maybe. But when you see the labor and craftsmanship that goes into something, can you really hate it?

I'm proud of this insight and want to tell her, but she isn't here. Again, she doesn't go running.

I try to read at night, but instead I think of her body, the shape of her.

Too many more nights like this, and I will go insane.

19 October

Where is she?

Robert and Klaus finish at three and drink beer in the fall sun. The leaves are yellow and beginning to fall. They invited me to join them, but I said no because what would I say to them? How will they understand me? I've spent years pretending and don't want to pretend anymore. I'm exhausted.

Every empty day takes me closer to Christmas. I asked

Robert about possibly working at the ranch next year, but he said a neighboring property manages it. If I take that job, I won't even be close to her anymore.

I went outside and looked down at her house. There are lights on, but no sign of Richard Eastman's car. That means she's there alone, just a few hundred feet away.

I want to go down and knock on the door with some excuse. I picture her pouring me a glass of wine and joining me on the sofa while Mozart plays on the stereo. We read each other lines from her favorite poems, and then...

Stop! I need to cut the shit. There's no point to these fantasies. Even if she is alone, I'll scare her away by turning up on her doorstep. And what if she has friends over? Her parents, even? Or what if Richard's car is in the shop and he's taken a taxi home? I might walk in on them together.

God, no! It's not possible.

I don't know the faintest thing about her, yet I know everything that matters.

But I need to be patient. Otherwise, I'll lose her forever.

20 October

The weekend arrives, and I'm woken at seven by Robert pounding on my door. I learned that there's a line in my contract that says they can make me work overtime whenever they want, including the weekends. The electricians are coming Monday, and he needs to prepare.

The work isn't bad. It's just Robert and me, which means I'm free of Klaus barking at me in accented English, but it also spoils my plans. I wanted to spend the day following her to plan my next move.

On my morning break, I see her biking down the driveway. I think about making an excuse and leaving—but it's not worth it. I won't catch her in time.

Robert cuts me loose at lunchtime. I take my scooter into town but don't see her anywhere. I go to the library and leave with *Romantic Poetry* and flip through it while I do my laundry.

A dog starved at his master's gate,
Predicts the ruin of the state...

My attention wanders. Even though I got A's in English, I never really liked literature. I prefer the certainties of mathematics over the paradoxes and strange pronouncements of these dead poets. I feel like I'm reading a book of old spells and incantations. It only has power if you're a true believer.

I buy a bottle of whiskey from the liquor store with my fake ID, hoping it might put me in a better state of mind to memorize these lines. Back at the estate, I sit outside and drink, but I still can't concentrate on the words.

Instead, I watch the house. She comes home late, followed soon after by Richard Eastman. He's taller than I expected and wearing a suit, even though it's a Saturday. He radiates power. I feel a desperate need to take it from him. People like me have nothing, just a single mother and a series of shitty stepdads, while people like Richard Eastman lazily inherit the world.

When he closes the front door, I hurl my glass onto the side of the mansion. It smashes and leaves a brown stain on the wood. I immediately regret my anger. That's not who I am, I tell myself. I pick up the glass and wipe the side of the house with my spare shirt, then go inside to get some water. I need to sober up.

He owns everything—the mansion, the smaller house, the ranch, the forest.

He has her, too.

But not for long, if I'm smart.

21 October

Nothing!

I woke late with a throbbing headache, sleeping hours past my alarm. I spent the day watching the house, but there was no sign of life till just before dark when I saw her return home.

I could describe what she's wearing, her shape, the way she moves—but that's not enough. I need more.

My weekend is gone. My hope is gone.

What can I do but wait for her? But how can I keep waiting?

I'm scared I will do something stupid out of desperation.

I won't write in this book until I see her again.

23 October

Finally—something. Not enough, but something.

Mrs. Eastman came through today to inspect the house. I saw her before she arrived, walking up the driveway. It was early, and Robert hadn't yet arrived.

I immediately sprinted to the stairs and heard her explain to Klaus that she wanted to see the view from the top. He commented that it was a building site and unsafe for visitors.

"Shall I ring my husband?" she asked.

I grinned and sprinted up to the top floor, knowing exactly where she was going—the living room with windows facing south, towards the town. Though we weren't working on this floor yet—the walls were open, ready for the electrician—I pretended to sweep.

"What are you doing here?" Klaus asked when she arrived.

"What does it look like?"

He grunted before turning to Mrs. Eastman. She was wearing leggings, running shoes, and an oversized woolen sweatshirt. Like last time, I could feel my hands shaking in her presence.

"As you can see, the place isn't safe for visitors."

She ignored him and walked to the window nearest me, looking out. The sun had just risen.

"Dear God, the very houses seem asleep," she muttered so only I could hear. Wordsworth again—she must still be reading the same book.

"And all that mighty heart is lying still," I countered before quoting another line I remembered from the same poem. "All bright and glittering in the smokeless air."

I caught her eye and saw something—curiosity but also fear.

"You like poetry?"

"What else is there?" I said, kicking the broom with my foot. "Though he's not my favorite."

"Who is?"

I glanced at Klaus, who was frowning at me with confusion and anger. "Alone, all alone, alone on a wide, wide sea."

"You think you're the ancient mariner?" She smirked. "I would have picked you more for Don Juan. 'That howsoever people fast and pray, the flesh is frail, and so the soul undone.'"

I found myself blushing and looked past her to the window. "I haven't read that one."

"Perhaps you don't need to."

Before I could ask what she meant, she nodded to Klaus and walked briskly out of the room. Klaus frowned at me. "What the hell was that about? Religious talk? Are you quoting the Bible or something?"

I just nodded and followed her out, aiming to catch up with her—but she was already jogging down the stairs. Before I was even at the landing, she was out the front door and running.

Why was she so quick to leave? The same reason she changed her routine and stopped running past the mansion in the afternoon.

She knows that I'm waiting for her, and she's scared.

15

VIRGINIA

The following week passes by slowly. I keep going into the trails every morning, but the routine is starting to drag, and I'm still spending most of the day in close proximity to Gillian.

Her music, the marijuana, the complete occupation of the living room. I used to think she was lazy, but now it feels like a special project. She can't possibly want to spend her days on the couch in this isolated ranch with no friends, no boyfriend, and no one except her phone and the TV. But still, she does it.

I can't quite figure her out—but I tell myself it's okay. At Christmas, we'll be moving into the main house, and I won't have to deal with her anymore. She can live here forever, for all I care. We can pay for her power and groceries as long as I can just pretend she doesn't exist.

On Thursday, I'm sitting on the porch outside. Aside from the line of perennials, the garden is mostly bare, the flowers and leaves all fallen, and the stems pruned back for winter. In the distance, the snow line is creeping down.

There's a dusting only a few hundred feet higher than the ranch, but the month has been unseasonably warm.

As soon as the ski fields open up, I will learn to ski. If Richard can pay for it, I'll go every day while he works. I'm the wife of a rich man, after all. It's time I started acting like it.

"Here, girl!" I make a face at the sound of PJ yelling at Casper. If she were my dog, I'd never say an angry word to her. "Get out of there!"

I walk around the side of the house to find Casper poking her nose under the roller door of the garage, which Richard didn't close properly when he left that morning. When she sees me, she gives me what I like to think is a cheeky grin before darting inside. PJ stands awkwardly a dozen feet away, clearly not wanting to follow.

"I'll get her," I call out, opening the roller door another foot higher and ducking inside.

I fumble for a light switch. The garage is empty except for a brand-new ATV sitting in the corner.

"What the hell?" I mutter, marching over to it. Richard hasn't got me a car yet—but he's somehow bought himself a new toy. I could kill him.

Casper trots over and licks my hand. I kneel down and pat her before noticing something else in the corner of the garage, next to Richard's gun safe.

A bike. I walk over to it and see it's a new mountain bike. Richard must have bought this for himself, too.

Too bad. Until I have a car, the bike is mine.

I lead Casper out of the garage and nod goodbye to PJ. When he's out of sight, I pack a bag, then wheel the bike down the gravel driveway to the road and take off.

The journey into town is mostly flat, but there are no

bike lanes around here, and the verge is either grass or rocks, so whenever a pickup or SUV speeds past, I find myself whispering a prayer. Most of them are fine, but every now and then, someone makes a point of giving me only a few inches of clearance.

When I get to Frostwood, I bike aimlessly through the streets until I find a coffee shop. I chain the bike to a pole and find an armchair near the door. I order a mocha latte and open my Kindle. I should be able to kill a few hours here, at least.

But just as my order arrives, I glance past the server and see my worst nightmare. Simone—sitting with a friend at the back of the shop. I consider abandoning my coffee just to avoid any awkward interaction, but a second later, her head turns, and we make eye contact. She gives me a nod, then waves me over.

Even though I'm technically her boss, I feel like a child summoned to the principal's office.

"This is Elsa," she says. "She wanted to meet you."

"Like the princess," I say before I can stop myself.

"Yeah, that's what everyone calls me," Elsa says. As she shakes my hand, I feel the callouses on her skin. I figure she's a gardener like Simone. "I'm a princess, all right."

Simone bursts out laughing, and I plaster a smile on my face, unsure of the joke. Elsa's lanky, with short brown hair sprinkled with gray—not precisely a Disney princess—but I feel there's some critical subtext I'm missing.

"Well, nice to meet you," I say, turning to leave.

"Hold up. Don't run off." Simone stands and gestures for me to take her seat. "I need to hit the head, so you may as well get to know each other."

As soon as Simone leaves, I feel Elsa's eyes on me. "You're gorgeous."

"Thank you."

"No, I mean it. Like, properly gorgeous. What a body. I bet you get hassled by men every time you leave the house."

I turn away from Elsa's hungry gaze. "Sometimes back in New York. Not so much around here. I've spent most of my time on the estate."

"That's right. You're on the Eastman Estate." She cackles with laughter. "What a joke. Like you're all lords and ladies. No offense. I mean, if anyone around here looks like a lady, it's yourself. But we're ranchers up here. The nobility were run out of this country centuries ago, and they ain't coming back. Not if I can help it."

She pats her ribs, and it's only then that I see the lump underneath her jacket. A handgun! The woman is packing heat to a goddamn coffee shop.

I look over my shoulder, praying that Simone will soon return.

"It must be a trip to live in that big house," she says, leaning in. It takes me a beat to realize that this is a question.

"Um, we're not living there yet. It's being renovated."

"Ha! Renovations." She laughs again, and the sounds remind me of the bark of a seal I once heard in the Central Park Zoo. "Nothing's ever good enough these days. But I guess you wouldn't want to live in the same house... after everything that happened. It would be a bit creepy."

I'm about to ask what she means, but when I see Simone arriving from the corner of my eye, I decide to escape.

"Nice to meet you," I say, and Elsa laughs again as if it's a joke.

Or, I think, as I walk back to my bike, is it more that *I'm* the joke?

16

VIRGINIA

When I get back, it's already dark, but Richard still isn't home. There's a strange smell in the house, even more potent than the usual cloud of marijuana.

I follow it to the kitchen to find the freezer wide open. There is a puddle of water on the floor and a strong smell of raw meat. I throw a pile of tea towels to soak up the water, then empty the freezer. There's a chicken, six steaks, and lamb chops—all soft and warm to the touch.

How long was I out? Only eight or so hours. They should still be cold, at least. This wasn't an accident. The meat wouldn't have defrosted in just one day, so Gillian must have switched the freezer off overnight or even defrosted them herself in the microwave.

I toss everything out, then storm into the living room. As usual, she's swiping through videos on her phone while the TV plays. When I come in, she smirks. She's expecting me; it's the highlight of her day. I shouldn't play into her hands, but I can't help it.

"What the hell did you do to the meat?"

She feigns confusion. "What are you talking about?"

"Someone left the freezer door open. The meat's ruined."

"I'm a vegan," she says, putting down her phone to stare at me. "It couldn't have been me."

I try to remind myself that this is a traumatized girl. Of all people, shouldn't I have sympathy for what she's going through? But the way she stares makes me want to slap her.

"That was supposed to last us for weeks."

"You can afford it," she says, shrugging. I watch as she picks up her phone and taps in her passcode in two straight lines: 147. 258.

"It's a mess," I say, searching for some sign of guilt or regret. Some normal human emotion, for Christ's sake.

But instead, she clicks on a podcast and puts in her head-phones. I recognize the title—it's a popular show about real world murder mysteries. "You clean it up," she mutters. "You're the maid, aren't you? It doesn't look like you do anything else around here. Except... you know."

Before I can think, I step towards her and slap the phone out of her hand. It smacks into the wall and lands on the carpet.

"What the..." she begins. But before she can finish, I pick up her ashtray of spent blunts and slam it into the glass coffee table, which cracks from corner to corner.

The shock on her face is quickly replaced by one of satisfaction. I've screwed up, and she knows it. Richard will see what I've done, and he'll take her side. I'm just glad I didn't hit her. I want to—but if I followed through, I might as well start packing my bags.

"You better hope my phone isn't cracked. You're such a psycho," she says.

As I leave the room, I wonder—how does she know?

17

VIRGINIA

Where did that come from?

I haven't done anything like that in years. But this wasn't my fault. This was her. Smashing the coffee table was just a normal human reaction to the kind of shit this girl is pulling. She's lucky I didn't shove her face into the glass.

Right?

I jog through the dark until I feel the anger subside. She won, but it shouldn't have been so easy. I had such high hopes when we moved to this beautiful place. I wanted a new life, a loving marriage, freedom, and peace. But here I am, trapped, friendless, alone, watching my marriage—and my mind—dissolve day by day.

My phone vibrates. Mom.

"Honey! I finally got through. How is it out there?"

I glance at the time. "What are you doing up? It must be nearly midnight out east."

"You know me."

It's a throwaway line, but the truth is, I do know her.

She's never been one to go to bed early if something more exciting is on offer, such as gossip, or wine, or men.

"It's beautiful," I say. "We're on a ranch near the glaciers. I'm walking outside now."

"Sounds like a great place to go on holiday," she says. "But a lonely place to live."

I remove the phone from my ear and give a silent scream. But it's my fault for answering. "This was right for us," I say, trying to keep the emotion from my voice.

"Listen, darling..." she begins, and I take a deep breath. I know exactly what's coming. "Are you sure about all this? I know he's stable and has money, but there's more to life. Really."

That's fine for you to say, I think. But not everyone can just sail through poverty with a smile on their face. After Dad died, we never had enough money. Every bill was late, every credit card maxed out for years. Mom never seemed to care.

I'm different, though. And the bills I have to pay dwarf anything Mom ever had.

"You can't say that. I just moved halfway across the country."

"That's my point, darling. You've isolated yourself. Do you think it's a good idea?"

I clench my fist at the subtext. Whenever I did something she disagreed with, Mom hinted that I was about to relapse.

"It's peaceful."

"I know you're worried about Steve, but that's ancient history. He's done his time. You did yours."

"He went to prison," I hiss. "I went to rehab. It's a little different, don't you think?"

"Well, they were both court-ordered, no?"

I shut my eyes in a pointless attempt to block out the

memories of that year. First, what Steve and I did in that apartment. Then, the police, the lawyers, the court case.

"That's ancient history. I'm with Richard now."

Her reply is so fast it's like she has it loaded in the chamber, ready to go.

"The debt collectors don't seem to think it's ancient history. Why hasn't Richard paid those off?" She clicks her tongue, even though she knows the answer. Richard doesn't know about my history as an addict. If he ever did find out, he'd be sure to leave me. "It's great that he's paid off your student loans. But that's no reason to marry someone."

"Mom! That's not fair."

"It's just... marriage is a partnership. And it seems like he's making all the decisions. He's further ahead in life, darling."

"He's not that much older."

I feel something furry pushing against my left hand and see Casper wagging her tail. I lean down and scratch behind her ears.

"Yes, but... you know. You need to have a partnership with an equal. That's what I did."

"Mom, I was an English major from a state school in massive debt. If I married my equal, I'd be renting a one-bedroom in Queens for the rest of my life," I said. "And honestly, I'd be lucky to be there. Steve was my equal. Did you want me to stay with him?"

"At least you would have some passion in your life! Not a damp squib."

"He's not a damp squib! He's just a real man with a real job. He's stable."

I find a stick on the ground and throw it as far as I can. Casper sprints after it gratefully.

"Darling, I don't want you waking up at fifty thinking you've slept away your life. You need passion. You only get one chance in this wild and precious life."

Mom had been throwing that Mary Oliver quote around my entire life. I used to find it persuasive, but now I wondered whether it was just an excuse to be permanently irresponsible.

"Yes, I've heard that one before. Was Dad passionate? Is that the wild and precious life you're recommending right now?" I ask. I'm going too far, but I can't help it.

"Yes, actually," she says quietly. "I've never been more alive than with your father."

I can't believe what I'm hearing. "Did you feel more alive when he threw you into the coffee table? Or when he threw a knife at your head? Or—"

She hangs up before I can continue. I instantly regret what I said, like I always do. Dad has been dead for nearly twenty years, and I can't keep blaming her for what happened. And she can't keep blaming me, either. His death —the best and worst thing to happen in both of our lives—is the backdrop to every conversation we have.

In the distance, I see a ride-on mower speeding along the grass. I watch as it climbs the hill towards the mansion and begins to go back and forth across the grass. There's something curious about how it focuses on such a small section of the property, so I go to take a closer look. As I walk towards the mower, I see Casper charging back.

"Hey, girl!" I say as she runs circles around me. I scratch her head and smile as she sprints back. As I get closer, the mower suddenly stops, and I see it's PJ. He's jogging towards me, Casper leaping at his side.

"How's your stay going?" he asks, panting.

"Great." I kneel and run my hands along Casper's back. "You're mowing the grass? Can't we pay someone to do that?"

"I like it. I was going to tell you there's a farmer's market in town. You might want to check it out if you're getting sick of the place."

"Thanks," I say, giving Casper another scratch. "God, you're beautiful."

"Thank you, ma'am."

I glance up at PJ and force a laugh. He's acting more friendly than he has since I moved in—though there's something about him that I find a little creepy. It's like he still thinks his family owns this land and we're just guests here. I also don't love the gun he has in a holster above his hips. Why does he have to be armed when he's out mowing the lawn? It must be a Montana thing.

"Anyway, I'll let you get back to it," I say, looking over his shoulders at the shapes in the grass. "What is that, anyway?"

As he protests, I step past him and walk up the hill.

"It's just kids from around here," he says hurriedly. "This place hasn't been much lived in for a while."

"Jesus," I say as I get closer. "Is that what I think it is?"

"It's nothing," PJ says, striding ahead of me. "Just a bit of weedkiller to leave their mark. Kids sometimes vandalize the place. There's a bit of poverty in the area..."

I squint. I know immediately that this isn't the work of local kids. There's only one person who would do this.

The letters aren't perfectly shaped, but the message is clear.

...EAVE BITCH.

18

VIRGINIA

s soon as I get in the front door, I hear Richard calling out from the kitchen.

"Where's dinner?"

No hello, no kiss on the cheek. I'm sick of it—I'm sick of the passive aggression of PJ and Simone, the irritability of Richard, and the outright bullying of Gillian. This whole place can go to hell.

"Ask your sister!" I yell, marching to my room and slamming the door behind me.

I hear laughter from the living room, followed by Richard's footsteps. A moment later, he opens the door and closes it quietly behind him. I recognize the posture immediately. This is Richard in executive mode, trying to calmly solve a problem.

That's what I've become: A problem to be solved, a human resource to be managed.

"What's going on, darling?"

I'm ashamed to admit that the kindness in his tone

makes me burst into tears. I wait for him to put his arm around my shoulder and comfort me, but he stays perched on the side of the bed.

"I've been trying not to tell you. I know she just lost her mom, and I know things are tricky... but she's making my life hell."

He frowns and opens his mouth to speak but then reconsiders. "I'm sure it's nothing."

"How the hell do you know it's nothing? I haven't even told you what she did."

He takes a breath as if he's dealing with an out-of-control child. "Go on, then. What has she done?"

"First, she put salt in my coffee."

"Virginia..."

"I'm just getting started. Then, she turned off the oven while I was cooking dinner. Remember that?" I hold up my hand to stop him interjecting. "Then, she put my underwear in with the wash."

At this, he laughs, making me want to reach across and slap him. "Those were accidents. How do you know she had anything to do with them?"

"I know!" I yell, though I'm starting to be aware of what this sounds like. He's right—I don't have any evidence. "She's been rude to me ever since she moved in. She left the freezer open and ruined all the meat. And then she burned a threat into the grass outside."

He's shaking his head again and smiling—that same condescending smile.

"PJ told me about that. He said it was kids."

"No!" I say. "It's her! I'm scared, Richard."

"She's a child." He stands up and makes to leave. "I'm on

your side, okay? But we need to give her the benefit of the doubt. You're being emotional. If you look at this objectively—"

"Objective! That's a joke." I scramble off the bed to stop him from leaving. "Look at what you're letting her get away with. She's smoking marijuana in our living room. After all the lectures you've given me about drug use. And after what happened with your mother..."

"Virginia!" he says, standing up. He's trying to warn me, but I'm too far gone to care.

"She's an addict, just like her. How can you put up with it? You've told me a million times that you despise addicts. And here she is, turning our house into a college dorm room."

"Enough!" He slams his fist into the wall like a hammer, leaving a dent in the cheap drywall. He looks back at the damage as if confused about where it came from. He's down the hallway a moment later, and I don't try to stop him. I hear the front door slam behind him.

There we go—another successful interaction in this happy marriage.

As I lie on the bed and try to calm down, I hear Gillian laughing from the hallway. Richard's right. Most of what she's done is a prank. But burning a message into the grass? That's taking things to another level.

At first, I thought she was just an obnoxious kid who was testing me. But now I'm wondering if something else is going on with Gillian.

Maybe I made a mistake trying to fight back. I don't know what she's capable of, and I'm scared I'm about to find out.

But in the back of my mind, there's one other possibility

I've been trying to avoid thinking about ever since he started texting me again.

What if it's not Gillian but someone exponentially more dangerous?

What if it's Steve?

19

VIRGINIA

The following day, I get up at the same time as Richard to avoid Gillian. I watch him change into his suit, then force myself into my running gear. When the front door closes, I go into the kitchen and pack food and water for the day. I still don't have a solution for Gillian, so I figure the best approach is just to stay out the entire day.

When I'm about to leave, I hear a knock at the front door, followed by a dog's bark. I go outside to find PJ standing with Casper restrained by a lead.

"Apologies for coming over this early," he says.

My eyes are drawn to the ever-present gun in his holster. For a moment, I wonder what he does with it on the toilet. I picture him wearing it in the shower and smile to myself.

"No problem. Always love to see my favorite girl."

He loosens the lead, and Casper comes across and licks my hand. I decide then and there to get a dog just like her—as soon as Gillian is gone.

"We had an intruder."

I look up in shock. "What do you mean?"

"A young man on the property."

"Ah, I saw him. He said he was a builder."

"No, ma'am," he said. "He's not on the crew up at the house."

I feel my phone vibrate. I check the message—it's a screenshot from Mom of my latest statement from Northcare Financial Solutions, the assholes that bundled up all my medical debt after I got out.

"What did he look like?"

"A bearded fellow, plaid shirt. Not a local, as far as I know."

"Hair color?"

He frowns and tilts his head slightly. "Are you expecting anyone?"

Mom texts again.

Why exactly can't he pay this off?

I put my phone away and shake my head. "Just want to be on the lookout."

"Light brown. Curly, past his ears."

Steve—could it be? Surely he hasn't found out where I live?

"Did you tell the police?"

"No police." He says it firmly as if to ward off any further objections. "We try not to bother law enforcement around here. We can take care of our own problems."

I feel a chill run through my body. What problems has this man taken care of on his own? "What do you mean?"

"I gave him the message," he says, patting his gun. "This ain't New York, ma'am. We can shoot trespassers on sight.

Shoot to kill. The police around here prefer it. Called the Castle Doctrine."

"Don't do that," I say hurriedly.

"Depends on the threat." He tips his hat like a cowboy in a saloon and leaves. I wonder if I have to worry about PJ, too. He swans around like he owns the place, probably because he feels like he does. It's been eighteen years since Richard was here, which means PJ's had the run of the property the entire time.

I'll speak with Richard about setting boundaries when the mansion is finished. I don't want PJ—or Gillian—on our land. I don't want wide open spaces. I want walls and gates with locks, security cameras, and alarms.

I walk outside, recognizing the way my anxiety is transforming into a panic. My doctor said I need to talk to someone I trust when this happens, so I call Richard's phone. He doesn't pick up, but that isn't unusual. His job often has him in back-to-back meetings all day.

But I need to talk to him. I'm worried about how I'll act if I return to the house and see Gillian.

How else can I get in touch with him? I search on my phone for the co-working space in town, but all the variations of 'Frostwood,' 'co-working,' and 'shared office' get me nowhere.

He must have rented his own space. I call his phone again—nothing. But then I get another idea. I search through my phone and find the number of Sandra McKenzie. Mrs. McKenzie, we always called her. Richard's secretary in New York. Even though he was working remotely, he would still need someone on his desk to manage his calendar.

"Arthur Power's office, GSP New York."

Powers? When I worked at GSP, he was the CFO. But maybe the secretaries had been reassigned?

"Hi, Sandra. It's Virginia Eastman."

"Virginia!" she squeals with surprise. "What a pleasant surprise to hear from you. How is Montana?"

"It's great. Gorgeous."

"I'm jealous. I can never leave the city. Grandkids, you know. But one day…" She pauses. "Sorry, hon, I have another call coming through. Is there anything I can help you with?"

"I was looking for my husband."

"Let me check his calendar." The line goes silent for a moment as she types into her computer. "Ah, it looks like he's taken a day off."

A day off? I saw him get changed into his suit this morning. "Are you sure?"

She pauses for just a second too long. "I must have my wires crossed. I was told he was on leave, but he might have been called into an executive meeting I don't know about. If you hold the line for a spell, I can ask—"

"No," I say quickly. I can hear my voice shaking. "No, sorry, I forgot. He's been out hunting, and I…"

I trail off, unable to keep the lie going. I hear her typing into her computer. "Okay, darling, I better go."

When she hangs up, I stare at the phone, hardly believing what she has told me. As I pack my bag, I try to keep the question from my mind, the question that—if answered—could ruin everything for me.

At rehab, they said that I need to avoid strong emotions to avoid a relapse, but here I am, having them all at once.

Panic. Fear. Anger.

But I can't help it. I have to know the truth.

What the hell is my husband really doing in Montana?

20

JAMES

27 October

I feel myself losing control. Today was almost a disaster. Maybe it was a disaster—I still don't know for sure. There haven't been any panicked phone calls from Robert, and no one has been banging on my door and telling me that I'm fired.

Yesterday, I told Robert that I won't work Saturdays and that I'll quit if he wants to force me. He must be sweating his Christmas deadline because even though he looks like he wants to rip out my intestines with his bare hands, he just nods. He'll make me pay for this in other ways, but it's okay.

I have my Saturdays.

Now, I have to make it count.

Today, I woke up early and had breakfast outside. It was overcast and cold, but with my coffee and toast, I was only slightly shivering—mostly from nerves because of what I had planned.

As I hoped, I saw Mr. Eastman leave around 8 a.m.—

though not in a suit this time but in camo gear and holding a rifle case. He drove off in a shiny pickup. I was glad to see that he was as much of an asshole as I had imagined. He's brought his young wife out to northern Montana, works twelve-hour days during the week, and then disappears on the weekends to go hunting.

She's practically a widow.

I waited an hour in case she planned to go out for the day. I packed a bag and was ready to jump on my scooter and follow her if necessary. But when she didn't surface, I went with the plan.

Stop pissing around.

Stop waiting for life to come.

Force it.

I strode down the hill, trusting that the speed of my descent would keep me moving forward, even though every instinct was screaming at me to turn back. My breathing was shallow, and my chest hurt as though I'd been sprinting.

My plan was simple: I would knock on the front door and ask if she wanted to come for a coffee. It was hardly a risk—with her husband away, she could do whatever she wished.

But as I approached the house, I saw that I was wrong. When I was less than a hundred feet away, the front door opened, and she began to run towards me with her hands out. As she got closer, I saw fear in her eyes.

"What the hell are you doing?" she said, breathless when she reached me.

"I..." I began, but I could not finish the sentence. As soon as I stood close to Mrs. Eastman, I saw that my vision of myself—a confident man with the charm and self-possession to seduce a lonely wife—was utterly absurd. I was just a boy.

"You've lost your mind," she said, looking past me. "He has cameras, you know. I'm sure of it. If you're caught coming down to the house, you'll lose your job."

"I wasn't—"

"Shut up," she said, but with a smile. "And I thought you were so articulate. I guess that's only when you're quoting other people."

I looked away, embarrassed. But this wasn't the disaster. Not yet. "I'm sorry. I was going to ask if you wanted a coffee."

"You have coffee in that building site?"

"French press."

"Fancy." She made a face to let me know it was anything but. "I guess that's worth a visit."

We walked up to the mansion in silence. I searched my brain for things to say, but everything that came to mind seemed boyish and silly next to a woman like her.

I led her to the kitchen and boiled a pot of water on the stove. She watched me the entire time, a faint smile on her face.

"Milk?"

She nodded. "What's your name?"

"James," I said. "What's yours?"

"You can call me Mrs. Eastman, thanks very much," she said flatly. I stared, feeling embarrassed again, and she laughed. "Sorry. That's not funny, is it?"

She told me her name as I pressed the coffee and poured it into a chipped mug.

"What should I call you?" I asked, leaning against the bench.

"When other people are around, call me Mrs. Eastman.

But my friends call me V. They think my name is too old-fashioned." She glanced around the filthy kitchen. "So you're living here?"

"Too expensive in town," I said.

"Must be lonely."

"I like it."

She stood up, and for a moment, I thought she was going to touch me. My body tensed, but she just walked out of the kitchen towards my bedroom.

"At least you've got a job," she called out.

"I hate it," I said, following her.

She glanced at me, frowning, and kept walking until she was at my door. She hesitated, then pushed inside. My mattress was unmade, my book of poetry splayed open alongside this diary. I wanted to snatch it away and ensure she didn't read it, but I somehow knew she would respect my privacy.

"Who are you?" She turned to me, frowning.

"I'm James," I replied, like an idiot.

"No, I mean, why aren't you in college? How many laborers—all of whom hate their job, by the way—spend their free time reading poetry?"

I knelt and arranged the books in a pile, with the diary at the bottom. "I've never been like other people," I said, my voice quiet. This wasn't going well at all. I was supposed to be masculine, confident, and in control. I was supposed to be seducing her, for Christ's sake. Instead, I responded to her questions like a schoolboy being interviewed by his principal.

"No. I can see that. But how did you even survive high school?"

"I've always been two people," I explained. "I kept my

real self a secret. You can't read poetry if you're a high school kid from rural Montana. So I played football, drank beer on weekends, went hunting."

"Dated cheerleaders."

"Yeah," I admitted.

"I bet they loved your eyes."

"Not just that," I shot back.

"You're quick."

I smiled, feeling more confident as I spoke. "I kept the other side to myself. I stayed up late reading the classics. I had knocked off Dickens at fifteen. Henry James. Then Woolf, Faulkner, the Romantic poets, Eliot, Yeats, Pound. I skipped ahead in math, too, and started to learn the basics of engineering. The teachers all thought I was a natural. But I worked harder than anyone."

"You must have got good grades."

"Summa cum laude."

"Christ almighty," she said with a laugh. "What are you doing here? Go to college."

"I'm taking a year off. People do it," I said with a shrug. "Anyway, who are you? I don't think every rich housewife around here walks around with copies of Wordsworth."

"This room is grim." I watched Mrs. Eastman—V—walk to the window. "I'm not who you think I am."

I walked up to her, close enough to touch. "Who are you then?"

As she turned to look at me, I thought I saw it in her eyes —the fear again behind her brash confidence. The fear and the desire.

So I kissed her. She held it briefly, and then the terrible thing happened. She tore away, furious.

"Don't ever—" she began, before sprinting out of the room.

And so, here I am, near midnight, still employed. Her husband hasn't barged in with his shotgun yet. If she was offended, she's keeping it to herself.

But she was not offended. It was an act. She knows that the kiss is a beginning, and she's scared.

She's not the only one.

21

VIRGINIA

The pharmacist squints into the computer for an age.

"Ah yes, we received your prescription from your doctor in New York. Come back in five."

The prescription took nearly a week to arrive, and I'm just glad I got here before the weekend.

I wander through the aisles, reading the claims of various kinds of vitamins. *If only it were that easy,* I thought. Just take a few vitamins, and be happy and healthy forever.

I hear a police siren outside and walk to the window. I peer past the cardboard cutouts and see a dozen people arguing with two burly cops. There's a sign that reads "Stolen Land, Broken Promises." It's a small protest, tiny by New York standards, but it feels charged, almost like the two sides hate each other.

Suddenly, one of the protestors strikes out at one of the cops. Within a second, he's hit by a taser and falls to the ground. Another of the protestors begins screaming as his face is slammed into the asphalt.

"Mrs. Eastman?"

I turn to the pharmacist, who is frowning slightly.

"That's something, huh?" I say, taking my medications. She holds onto the package for a second before handing it over.

"We only have two weeks' supply in stock, so you'll have to come back," she says. "Once a day with food. If you miss a day, then wait." She runs through the side effects with the same look of concern. "Are you new here?"

"Yeah, I moved from New York a few days ago. Eastman Estate. A few miles north."

"Ah, of course. Didn't put it together from your name. I know the place." She pauses for a moment as if she wants to tell me something else about my medication, but I'm tired of being treated like an invalid.

"Where's the co-working space?"

"Huh?"

"My husband said he's at the co-working space. Like a shared office for startups? I thought I'd see where it is."

She suddenly laughs, and I get the feeling I'm being mocked. "This ain't New York City, darling. We barely have a coffee shop in the off-season. Got to go to Missoula for that kind of thing."

I stare at the half-empty bottle of anti-anxiety meds while she rings up the bill. Every year, it gets more expensive —and despite being married to a millionaire, my debts aren't moving. Richard paid off my student loans not long after we married, but the interest on my debts is eye-watering. Unless I can find a way to increase my allowance, it will stay that way.

When Richard first suggested giving me an allowance, I was insulted—until I realized I could use the money to pay down my debt secretly. When he suggested a grand per week, I quickly agreed. But when I ran the calculations, I realized that a grand a week would barely cover my interest, let alone any other expenses I was expected to incur.

The designer dresses. The heels. The flawless appearance to impress his colleagues and friends in New York.

I went off the meds just before coming to Montana. For some reason, I thought all the anxiety I felt in New York would fall away when I went out west. But now it's worse— almost as bad as anything I've ever experienced.

Almost, but not quite. But I can feel that same sense of the world slipping away, of my thoughts getting so loud that they make it impossible to live a normal life. Richard's wrong about Gillian, but when I think about how I slapped the phone out of her hand, I realize I'm still not being myself.

Outside, I take a pill and then ride aimlessly through the quiet streets of Frostwood. There's no sign of a farmer's market, and I wonder if PJ made that up to get rid of me. Not that it matters. I'm not going home until I'm sure Richard is back. I want to talk to him again about what Gillian did to the lawn. She must have poisoned the grass—no small feat. I won't let him just ignore what she's doing.

The road I'm on suddenly ends, and I find myself on a path next to a river. I park my bike and scramble down the bank to the water's edge. I take off my shoes and sit with my feet in the freezing water, enjoying the shock of it. That's the funny thing about being human: How we see the world can change in an instant.

From a distance, the mountains seem so permanent, though I know that up close, they're full of disturbances, slips, landslides, fallen trees, and swollen rivers. That's what you don't see in the postcards—the permanent movement of life and death.

I grimace. There I am again, being a bad poet.

I glance across the river, then suddenly scramble behind some vegetation.

He's here. The last person I want to see.

Steve—I'd recognize those curls anywhere. He's strolling along, staring at his phone. A few seconds later, I feel my phone vibrate.

> We belong together. Why can't you see that?

I keep still, praying that he doesn't look across the river. I know immediately that it was Steve that PJ found on the property. He not only found out that I'm in Montana, but he's also followed me here.

He wouldn't do that without a reason. Or, more to the point, without a plan.

Between Gillian and Steve, I would have to watch my back.

22

VIRGINIA

When I get off my bike at the estate, I run through all the texts that Steve has sent me since he first got my number over a month ago. I haven't responded once, but that hasn't stopped the steady stream of messages.

How did he find out where I am?

There's only one possible culprit.

I quickly scrawl a text to Mom.

> Did you tell Steve where I live?

Within a second, she responds with a simple thumbs-up emoji.

I write back.

> Are you crazy? He's insane!

This time, she responds with a wink-face and writes:

Takes one to know one.

I type a curse-laden response and then delete it. Whenever I insult Mom, she forces me to go over it with her in so much detail that I apologize just to get free.

As I park the bike in the garage, Casper bounds up and drops a stick at my feet. I throw it. I try to concentrate on the beautiful animal and not all the memories that Steve has brought back.

What we did that night.

Why he ended up in jail, and I ended up in rehab.

I'm not a monster, I tell myself. I'm not really a psycho. But then, why did we do it? I squeeze my eyes shut and try not to rehash the reasons. Over the last decade, I've forgotten almost everything that happened that night.

Almost.

I kneel and pat Casper again. She has a low belly, and I figure she can't be much of a working dog. Maybe PJ's property isn't large enough to give her a workout.

"She's beautiful."

I squeal in fright to see a man beside me. In the light of the moon, I can see that he's tall and lean, clean-shaved, and boyishly handsome.

"Thanks..."

He bends down to pat Casper, who licks his hand. I recognize him as one of the builders working in the house.

"Sorry, I didn't mean to disturb you. Just an admirer."

Before I can say anything, he's running off. Part of me wonders if he should go around our property after hours. But the other part of me just wants to watch him.

There's a piercing whistle, and Casper trots towards the mansion, where PJ is standing. I follow behind until I'm a few dozen feet away and see what PJ is doing. He's scrubbing furiously, but whatever it says—painted on the walls in red, three feet high—isn't coming off.

I go closer until I can make out the words.

LAST WARNING.

PJ stops working and looks at me. I know he's about to give his usual excuse and say it's teenagers, but I also know he doesn't believe it. This isn't a random act of graffiti. It's Gillian again.

I can't live like this, I think to myself as I walk back to the house.

Something has to be done.

23

VIRGINIA

Walking back towards the house, I think of the Byron poem "Darkness." One day, the sun burns out. People burn all the candles, then all the trees, then everything they own, until nothing's left. It's one of the few poems that's ever given me nightmares.

Is that my life? Are all the bright things slowly being used up? Will I soon be sitting alone in the black?

The bright sun was extinguish'd, and the stars
Did wander darkling in the eternal space.

"Where have you been?"

Richard is sitting in the kitchen, staring at a laptop screen. Tired and sweaty, I fall into the seat beside him. As soon as I see his screen, he closes the lid.

"Riding my bike," I say.

"Alone?"

"Who else would go with me?" I say with a scoff. "I don't know anyone else here. I'm basically living alone."

He puts his head in his hands as if my comment has caused him great hardship, but I continue. After what I learned from Sandra from GSP, I'm not in the mood to appease him. Maybe I should if I'm being strategic. But I'm tired and angry, and I don't give two shits about strategy anymore.

"Why did I come here if I never see you? You know I didn't want to come. I had a life. I have family back east."

"You know it wasn't working. We needed a fresh start."

"We!" I say with emphasis, reaching across to take his hand. "I came here to be with you."

"I'm still working. You know my job. It's very demanding."

I drop his hand but choose not to confront him. I'm not ready yet. As soon as I do that, our entire relationship will crumble. He'll forever be a liar.

The rivers, lakes and ocean all stood still,
And nothing stirr'd within their silent depths.

I need to pretend for a little longer until I know the truth and have a plan.

"You work hard. But at least in New York, I wasn't surrounded by people who want to hurt me."

"What do you mean?"

"The graffiti? Did PJ tell you about the latest addition?"

"What about it?" He gives me a dismissive scoff. "PJ said it's just kids."

"If he's so confident about his theories, he should put up cameras. Then we'd catch her." My fingers tap the table with increasing violence. "It's Gillian. You have to see it. You know how she's acting."

"She wouldn't do that."

"You don't even know her!"

He puts his laptop under his arm and stands. This is text-book Richard—he runs from conflict before it escalates. It works, in a way. Sometimes, I wonder if we'd still be together if he were a man who expressed himself honestly.

"I don't want security cameras on my property. That's a non-starter." I smile inwardly at the corporate speak. "This is my home. Anyway, it's not Gillian. I can promise you that. She's my sister."

"I feel like I'm losing my mind." I'm on my feet, too—though I can't remember standing. "You just met her for the first time! You don't know what she's capable of. I can't believe you don't see it."

He leaves without responding. I stand at the kitchen sink and splash water on my face. I feel a tension in my brain, the heat of my thoughts. I came here for stillness and boredom, for beauty and peace. But I can feel that old intensity, the fire starting to rage once again. The last time I truly let it rage, my life shifted forever. Steve went to jail, and I lost everything. I'm only just regaining my footing. I need to fight it—even though part of me wants to let go, once and for all.

The waves were dead; the tides were in their grave.

I pray that the medications do their job and I can start to think straight again.

As I take a drink of water, I see someone standing in the doorway. It's Gillian, grinning to herself. She hears everything and knows that she is winning. She's breaking up our marriage, and she's chasing me away.

Gillian. You don't know me at all. I never run. I fight.

To hell with the consequences.

24

VIRGINIA

I'm having breakfast when there's a knock at the door. I smooth down my hair, wondering who would visit this early. There's been no one since we moved in—no neighbors or friends of the family. I picture an elderly woman holding an apple pie to welcome me to Frostwood, but the fantasy dies when I see the too-familiar outline of PJ.

"It's early," I say, opening the door. Despite the cold morning, he's only wearing a flannel shirt and jeans. As always, there's a handgun on his hip. I still find it strange, though now that I know Steve is around, it's nice to know someone is guarding the property.

"Apologies for the intrusion. Just delivering the mail." He hands me a stack of envelopes held together by a rubber band. "Just cleared out the box in town."

"We don't get mail here?"

"Your husband set it up," he says, his tone becoming sharper. I'm being rude, but I can't help it—there's still something about this man that I don't trust. "Take it up with him."

Before I can close the door, he hands me a newspaper. "Richard also ordered the paper from Missoula delivered every morning. Today's the first issue."

I nod, then close the door.

As I flip through the envelopes, I feel my knees go weak. This is what I've been trying to ignore for months. Bills—stacks of them, all forwarded from Mom.

I open the latest and stare at the numbers, not quite believing that they could be real. The bills from the lawyer and my court-ordered stays in rehab, with all the interest piled on, is approaching half a million dollars. I could work my entire life and only chip away at the principal.

All because of one stupid night.

Or was it one stupid relationship?

I stack the bills in a line, chop them in half with a pair of scissors, and then bury them in the trash under the scraps from breakfast.

Richard's being an asshole, and Montana has become a beautiful nightmare. But I have no option but to stay. He was the only person in my life who could bail me out. One day, I'd get access to his money and be able to pay it off. All at once. Freedom.

What would that feel like? I've been walking around with this albatross for so long that I've forgotten what it's like to be someone with real choices.

But for now, there's no plan B. It's Richard or a mountain of debt.

After breakfast, I go to the garage and ride the bike into town. I've stopped asking Richard about the car. He keeps telling me he ordered it, but somehow, I feel he wants to keep me trapped here on the ranch. Not so he can watch me —but so I can't watch him.

Since I found out about his secret day off, I've been tracking his late nights, his mysterious hunting trips, his "meetings with Asia."

How many of them are lies?

And more to the point, what the hell is he doing when he's not working?

I spend most of the day riding through the trails around the outskirts of town, stopping only to grab lunch at a diner. I figure if I keep moving, there's less chance of Steve creeping up on me. Demanding that I leave Richard. Demanding that I keep the promises I made more than a decade ago when we were both just kids.

I can remember the last conversation we had before we were arrested.

"Promise that you'll wait for me."

"Of course." I can still feel the hot tears running down my face. "I'll wait forever."

"I'll be out before you know it. We can have a family together. I love you."

"Forever," I repeated.

Now, the words seem so absurdly melodramatic. They feel like they were pulled from a soap opera. These are the vows of children. No one would expect me to keep them.

No one, that is, except Steve.

When I get home, I hear Richard's voice from the kitchen.

"Finally!"

My legs feel like jelly as I walk to the kitchen. I must have biked forty miles today. I just want to have a shower and collapse.

"Surprise!"

"What's this?" I say with a grin. I thought I'd have to

cook, but a Thai chicken salad is already served in my place. Richard is sitting in front of a generous serving of roast beef and potatoes.

"I thought you deserved a night off." He leans across and kisses me on the mouth. "I know it's been hard for you."

I stare at the food like it's a puzzle I need to solve, then look up and see the bags on the bench. This is all high-end takeaway—but it's still an unexpected gesture.

"Go on, eat!"

"I need a shower."

"You look fine to me."

As I eat, he tells me about a deal they've closed in the Middle East worth tens of millions of dollars, beating out the biggest engineering companies in the world.

When we finish, he tells me to go shower while he cleans up.

"That machine next to the sink is called a dishwasher," I say before letting out a squeal as he whips me with a dish-towel. "Hey!"

I'm still laughing as I pass the living room, where Gillian is staring at her phone. Dark circles are under her eyes, and I wonder if her lifestyle is catching up with her. I never see her eat anything; as far as I know, she never even leaves the house. She's surviving on a diet of weed and energy drinks.

As I shower, I think about the threatening messages she's left. She's trying to scare me away—but why? What's the point? It's gone beyond bullying. It's pathological. I just need Richard to see the truth.

I come out of the bathroom wearing a towel, and a second later, I feel someone wrap their arms around my waist. It's been so long since I've been touched that I cry out, but the arms hold me tighter.

"Richard?" I say, feeling his lips on my neck—and something else pressing against my lower back.

"Don't talk."

He pulls away my towel, leads me to the bed, and then undresses. We kiss for a few seconds, and then he reaches across the bed and fumbles through the drawer.

"What are you doing?" I ask.

He kneels above me on the bed, fumbling with something in his hands—a condom. I reach out to stop him.

"I thought we could..."

He pulls his hand away and rolls it on. "Not yet."

I want to argue, but before I can say a word, it's too late. He's in me, on top of me, his face buried in the pillow above my shoulder, moving at pace.

"Richard..." I whisper. I want him to slow down, to kiss me, to touch me. But he keeps his head buried until the end when he finishes with a shudder.

He rolls off, panting. I turn away and face the wall, not wanting him to see my disappointment. I knew that this whole night had been a chore for him. The dinner, the sex, the forced lightheartedness—it's all a strategy to be successfully executed. He wanted the fights to end, and he thought this would do it.

"I want a child," I say.

When he doesn't respond, I turn over and see that the bed is empty and he's already gone.

25

JAMES

29 October

Nothing.

I decide not to sit outside after work, watching for her. That's not enough for me anymore.

What if she told her husband what happened? What if he's making plans to kill me?

No! There's no point worrying about ridiculous fears when it seems like my biggest fear is real. She didn't want me to kiss her. I offended her. She might not tell anyone because it's too humiliating to be kissed by the boy apprentice. But she'll avoid me for as long as I work here.

I'll never see her again.

30 October

My mother calls me on my cell phone, which still has the numbers of all my high school friends. I get texts every now and then, but I don't respond to anyone—except Mom.

I spend a minute telling her what I'm doing, and she spends the next hour ranting about the hardships of her life. The lack of money and dignity. She tells me in great detail how it all went wrong, the same story she's told me my entire life.

A few minutes into the call, I realize that she's high. I recognize from my childhood an uneven, rambling rhythm to her speech.

She had been clean for nearly a year this time.

I interrupt to tell her that she's still young. She had me when she was seventeen, so she's only in her mid-thirties. She has more than half her life in front of her. She could go to school, start a new career, and build a new life.

But I don't know why I try. Every time I make these suggestions, she takes them like bullet wounds to her gut. It makes her cry with anguish and focus even more on the injustices that led her to the wrong neighborhood, the drug habit, the kid—me—an albatross around her neck.

When I hang up, I'm exhausted and angry. She's right. The world isn't fair.

The problem is that she never tells me what I'm supposed to do about it.

1 November

Another empty day. I wait for her to find an excuse to visit the mansion, but it doesn't happen. I know she hasn't told anyone—but can I be sure of anything else?

I kissed her; she kissed me back. But that doesn't mean anything.

The work is getting easier on my body but somehow harder on my mind. The days are empty and long. I check the big clock in the kitchen multiple times a day, but the hours never pass as quickly as they should.

I think about getting her number—maybe going through the documents in Robert's project office after hours until I find it—but I know it's a bad idea. It would either scare her away or leave a trail of evidence for her husband.

What can I do? I need to know, one way or another. If she truly hates me, then I'll need to leave. If I don't find out how she feels soon, I'll do something crazy.

26

VIRGINIA

I walk down to the gate and get the newspaper. Another week has gone by. On the weekend, Richard took me into Frostwood for coffee, and then we drove up to inspect his cabin, which had just been cleaned. The snow cover was still light, and Richard predicted a mild season. I wanted to stay the night so I could see the stars, but he said that he had to work on Sunday.

We don't talk much, but when we do, it's about the estate, the town, how beautiful it is in this part of the world—everything except what's important.

His sister and her threats.

My need for a baby.

Our future in this place.

He came home after I was asleep on Sunday night and was gone when I woke up this morning. I still haven't found out what he's doing outside of work. Part of me wants to ignore it until I'm pregnant. Because if I find out the truth, I might have to make a decision about our marriage. And I'm not ready to give up on my dreams just yet.

I love him, I say to myself as the coffee machine grinds away. He's my soulmate. After this rough patch, I'll have a lifetime of peace. Family, money, beauty—what else do I need?

I sit outside and skim through the paper. It's about a quarter of the size of the *Times* and is more conservative than I'm used to, but at least it brings me closer to the community. I read about state politics, farm subsidies, the ski season, the problems with local schools, and football. I try to make myself care about all of it.

About halfway through, I notice that certain words have been circled.

If. Going. You.

I go back to the start of the paper and write them down on a notepad. When I finished the whole sentence, I stand up with a jolt. My coffee cup falls from the armrest to the deck, the handle snapping off, the brown liquid pooling on the timber like a chemical spill.

If you stay here, I'm going to murder you.

I pick up the notepad and stare at the words—and the longer I stare, the less scared I am. This isn't what real murderers do, I tell myself. Real murderers just *murder* people. They don't waste weeks of their life messing with them.

The message feels unreal, like I've just stepped into a bad murder mystery. And who do I know that listens to bad murder mysteries?

A few seconds later, I push open Gillian's door without knocking. She's curled up in a ball, clutching a small, faded teddy bear.

"This is super original," I say, throwing the newspaper at her head. "Just so you know, I'm not scared of your threats."

Gillian pushes the newspaper away and rubs her eyes. "Crazy bitch. What are you doing?"

"The paper. You're threatening me."

She sits up, blinking. "What are you talking about?" If I didn't know better, I'd say she almost looks worried.

"This." I toss her the notepad.

She stares at the message, then looks up at me, frowning. "You're going to murder me? I'd like to see you try."

As I march across the room, she lets out a squeal, but I just grab the newspaper away and show her one of the words that has been circled.

"Don't act dumb. I found this in the paper this morning. I don't know how you did it, but you underlined these words before I got up."

She flicked through the pages, pausing when she got to the word 'murder.'

"Jesus..."

"I don't believe this act," I say, shaking my head. "Not for a second. You might as well not bother."

She folds the paper up and holds it out for me to take. "I didn't do this."

"Bullshit," I say, snatching it back. "You've been messing with me ever since I arrived."

I wait for her to deny that, too, but she just nods. "Yeah. But this isn't me. I promise. You'd have to be crazy to do this." I keep staring at her until she waves me away. "Fine. I don't care if you don't believe me. You'll find out when this psycho kills you for real."

"You'll pay for this," I say before leaving the room and slamming the door as hard as I can.

It was her, I tell myself, as I pick up my mug from outside. *Please, God, let it be her.*

27

VIRGINIA

PJ knocks on the door for another mail delivery a few hours later. "I was in town," he grunts, almost as if he's apologizing. Before I can say a word of thanks, he's walking back to his truck.

I see more bills forwarded from Mom. The mountain of debt grows a few feet higher. I cut the envelopes in two without opening them and toss them in the trash.

This can't go on. We need to have an honest conversation before I lose my mind.

I take out my phone and call.

Before I met Richard, I had planned on filing Chapter 7 bankruptcy. It would make my life harder through my thirties, but at least it wouldn't follow me throughout my life. But now that I'm married, it'll be a lot more complicated.

I could just confess, of course. Tell him that I went to rehab before college. They thought I was an addict because my lawyer said that was the smartest move. I looked like an innocent white girl from the suburbs, which made it easy for the judge to feel like I wasn't responsible for my actions.

It was Steve. Steve and the drugs.

Bullshit, all of it.

If I confess, he'll divorce me. But the courts might make him pay down my debts. Or he might pay them to avoid the legal fees.

But I can't tell Richard because I'm not just worried that he'll find out about rehab. I'm worried that he'll find out the whole story. The real reason I went to rehab and Steve went to prison.

The promises I made—the debts I'll never be able to clear.

To my surprise, Richard answers after only a few rings.

"What's up?" he asks, his voice clipped and businesslike. He's clearly not in the mood to chat—but too bad.

"We need to talk."

"Now?" I hear a woman's voice in the background. I wonder if he's there right now, at her house. Maybe he's pissed off because I've interrupted a session of vigorous lovemaking.

"Who's that?"

"Huh?" The voice grows softer, then I hear the sound of a door closing. "Sorry, it's a bit loud at the office."

Office—I remember what the pharmacist had said. Is this another one of his lies?

"Where's your office? It's a co-working space, isn't it?"

"Virginia... I have work to do."

"I just want the address. Just in case there's an emergency."

"Seriously?" He lets out a sigh. "I'll text it to you, okay? Is that all?"

Is it all? I feel like I'm standing in front of a wide ravine, and the only way forward is a rickety old bridge. I can sit and wait here forever, but the facts aren't going to change. There's only one way forward, and it could be disastrous.

"I want to go back to New York."

As soon as the words leave my mouth, I know it's true. With Gillian and Steve, the pranks and the threats, I can't stay here any longer.

"I hope you're kidding." His voice is a low growl, almost threatening. "I've moved my whole life out here. I'm spending a million dollars renovating the house. It's out of the question."

"But—"

"It's a non-starter, Virginia. You've been here a few weeks. You can't just decide that." There's a loud thump, which sounds like a fist slamming onto a table. "With all the shit I'm dealing with—"

"What about all the shit I'm dealing with?"

"She's a child!" He curses. "And you're a child if you can't deal with her. You want babies, and yet you can't even handle three weeks out here."

I open the newspaper and look through the circled words once more. I want to tell him what she's done, but I know how he'll respond.

She's just a kid.

Her mother had just died.

And all the rest.

"I'm not happy."

He's quiet for a moment, but when he talks, his voice is elevated and passionate. "Happy? Who said anything about happiness? I'm building something real here. We're building entire cities in the Middle East. Did you know that? And you ask about happiness while my team is reshaping the world...

I thought you were tougher than this." I'm about to respond when I hear a door open. There's a voice again—the woman. "I have to go. We have the UK on the line."

"Who is that?" I demand, my voice loud and shrill, but he's already hung up.

28

VIRGINIA

It's time for the truth—and there's only one way to get it.

The night before, I go to bed in my clothes. I sleep fitfully, my mind plagued by strange theories about Richard. He claims to be busy, but what does he do all day?

Is he setting up a rival company? Working secretly with a competitor?

Maybe it's something illegal. Running drugs for the cartel. Insider trading. Fraud or embezzlement.

Or maybe he's sleeping with another woman—or women, plural. I picture him attending an orgy, servicing a dozen women at once, all in the throes of ecstasy.

None of that seems like Richard. He's a million miles from being Don Juan. Sleeping with multiple women would make him more exhausted than excited.

That's the problem, then: Nothing I can imagine seems likely, which leaves one final scenario—the most likely but also the saddest.

I don't know my husband.

When we met, he was already an executive. I was a lowly communications assistant assigned to help him speak at a conference in London. We worked well together. He was humble and gracious and had a reputation for being one of the few execs at the company who didn't blow a gasket in meetings.

The only time I saw any passion was when I told him I didn't drink. He went on a rant about the downsides of alcohol. The following day, he invited me on a hike in Epping Forest, an hour from where we stayed in the City of London. He spent most of the time talking about the evils of the pharmaceutical industry. I didn't probe but guessed that a family member had been addicted to painkillers. I learned later that it was his mother.

We ate lunch beside a stream, and it was there that he recited a poem.

While giant London, known to all the world,
Was nothing but a guess among the trees,
Though only half a day from where we stood.

"John Clare," I said, vaguely remembering the lines from university. "You read poetry?"

He shook his head shyly. "I memorized it from a website. Someone at work said you studied poetry at college, so I thought I'd impress you. Not sure if that's actually impressive, of course. But it's about Epping Forest."

Without thinking, I leaned across and kissed him. I quickly pulled away, panicked, but then he pulled me close and kissed me back. We made out several more times on the walk back through the forest. After dinner that night, I stayed in his hotel room. He upgraded my flight to first class, and we were officially announced as a couple to HR the following week.

The following months were a whirlwind. It didn't take long for me to move out of my shoebox in Queens to his massive apartment on the Upper West Side.

He proposed to me six months after that first kiss.

It sounds romantic when you give the short version. But in the extended version, those moments of romance were just islands in an otherwise empty sea. He worked intensely long hours, and the truth is, I hardly ever saw him. When I did see him, he was usually dead tired. In the beginning, I spent time with my friends, but once I was on the Upper West Side, the trajectory of my life suddenly felt so much different than theirs. I stopped going to the cramped dinners in tiny apartments and the drinks in dive bars.

And then, of course, I stopped getting invited.

I was sad to leave my friends, but I thought it would be worth it to start again, free at last.

I'm woken by the vibration of my watch at five. I lie awake until he gets up half an hour later. I listen to him shower and brush his teeth, and wait for him to gently close the front door.

When it finally shuts, I pull on my shoes and go to the window. He's running—great. If he were taking the car, I'd have to figure out another way, maybe a GPS. But I prefer this—low-tech and immediate.

After he disappears down the dark driveway, I leave the house to get my bike and follow him from a distance. He's wearing a backpack, which I assume has his clothes for the day. There's a slight crunch of my tires, but it's quiet once we're on the road. There are no streetlights out here, so I let him get a few hundred feet ahead—far enough for him not to recognize me if he turns around.

There are only a few turns off the road out here, so it's

easy to follow his route. He keeps going for nearly an hour at a steady pace until he turns off about a mile from town. I pause at the corner as streetlights are now illuminating the road. I watch him jog past a row of small lifestyle properties, each with substantial houses near the road and one or two paddocks behind.

The road curls around, and I lose track of him. I get on my bike and pedal, and when I get to the corner, I see him running down a path. Number 29. It's a beautiful dark wooden house with three levels. I see three brown horses milling about near the fence in the paddock outside. Behind the house, a few sheep and llamas are munching quietly on the grass.

I jump with fright as a car zooms past. I hear car doors opening and slamming shut across the road. It's getting light, and I'm a stranger on a quiet road, the kind of place where everyone knows everyone.

I can't stay long. But I can't leave without some idea about what he's doing. I look around anxiously until I see a large juniper tree on the border of the property. Perfect. I take out my phone and start recording, then carefully balance it in the branches of the tree to face the house. The phone is fully charged, so I should get at least a few hours of footage.

I'm about to return to my bike when I hear voices nearby. Too close—the voices are coming from the house. Without thinking, I scramble under the branches of the juniper tree. From this angle, I can't see anything. The voices go further into the distance, towards the paddocks. A few minutes later, they return. Through the thick canopy of branches, I see a blonde head—a woman.

I wait a minute, then commando-crawl back onto the

grass. I'm lucky that there's no one else around. I grab the phone, jump on my bike, and return to the main road towards town. I find a coffee shop and take a table in the corner before finally taking out my phone.

This is it—the truth.

I click on the video with shaky hands. The picture shows half the house and a slice of the paddocks. There's nothing for a minute, and suddenly, the blonde enters the frame. She's gorgeous—younger than me but more put together. She's wearing tight blue jeans and boots and is carrying a bucket. She makes her way down to the paddock and then whistles. The horses come running over, and she tips something onto the ground for each of them.

Next to her, a girl of four or so is whispering to the horses. She pets one of them on the nose. I watch the scene three times, hypnotized by what it represents. This isn't an office but a family home.

I feel a thrum of jealousy ripple through my body. This looks like more than an affair. This is domestic bliss. This is everything I want for us—and he's already getting it elsewhere.

I already know that I won't let him get away with it.

29

JAMES

2 November

Will I ever know?

Today, I tried my best to find out. Robert was off sick, and Klaus decided to take the day off, so I had the entire Friday to myself. I took my coffee outside and watched the sun rise over the estate. It was a beautiful still day—perfect for what I had planned.

She left mid-morning on her bike. I immediately jumped on my Suzuki and followed her onto the road. She was going slowly, barely 15 miles an hour, and it didn't take her long to figure out someone was following her. About a mile down the road, she pulled over and stared at me defiantly.

When I stopped and took off my helmet, her mouth fell open.

"You!" She stepped across to hit me, hard, in the shoulder. I stumbled and almost fell off my scooter. "What the hell are you doing?"

Her voice had real anger—but I was angry, too.

"Why haven't you come to see me?"

"What a question! You're lucky I didn't tell my husband." She pokes me in the chest. "You're lucky you still have a job."

"Why haven't you come to see me?" I said again.

She stepped back and rolled her eyes. "You're such a child."

"No, I'm not. Why—"

"Stop! Are you insane or just stupid? You know why." She rubbed her lips, but when she spoke again, the anger was gone. "Really, James. What do you want from me? I'm married."

I smiled at her. We both knew what I wanted. "Come with me."

"On my bike? I don't think so. I can't keep up."

"Then hop on."

"Without a helmet? Why?" She was trying to stay mad at me, but I could tell it was just a performance. "Where are you going?"

I held out my hand. "A hike to a special place."

She stared at it for a moment, then shook her head. "Let me lock up my bike first."

A minute later, I was driving slowly through the country roads of northern Montana towards the mountains. I had a route planned that I'd copied from a local guidebook.

By the time we parked at the trailhead, miles from any sign of human life, we were covered in white dust from the roads.

"You look ridiculous," she said, wiping her eyes.

"Speak for yourself."

"And I'm freezing." I unzipped my jacket, and she laughed. "Chill out, Don Juan. I'm not looking for any grand romantic gestures. Let's just get moving. Did you bring enough water for both of us?"

The hike was more difficult than I thought. We climbed for the first two hours, miles into the foothills. V was much fitter than me and made jokes whenever I asked for a break. By noon, the sun was baking down, and as we left the tree line, we were both sweating heavily. We passed through a large clearing. On the other side, I pushed through a patch of overgrown forest.

"Where are you taking me?" she asked. "Is this even a marked trail?"

I checked the map I had ripped out of my diary. "Not maintained after a storm last winter. But it's worth it."

"I hope you're not planning on murdering me," she said. "They'll never find the body out here."

After another hour of walking, I began to doubt myself. It would be terrible luck if we got lost and couldn't return to the scooter before dark. But just when I thought about giving up, the trail finally ended, right onto the sandy beach of a small lake.

"Wow," she said, kicking off her shoes and collapsing on the sand. "This is something."

"Don't stop now," I said. "You have to come in. While you're still hot."

I stripped off my shirt and shorts.

"You're kidding," she said. "It must be freezing."

"In a month or two, it literally will be," I said, taking a beat before stepping out of my underwear and into the water. I could feel her eyes on my body. I'm lean and muscled—not just from the work at the mansion but from years of football workouts. Girls always liked my body. Now, it was time to see if a woman would, too.

I went under the water with a yell and swam out for a few feet before surfacing. When I turned to face her again, she was already in the water. I caught a glimpse of her breasts before she dove under. I decided not to try anything —we'd only kissed once, after all, and I'd barely touched her —but I soon felt her arms around my stomach.

"This was a terrible idea," she said before kissing me. "Shit. Jesus Christ, you are a genuine maniac. I'm covered in goose pimples."

"Me too." I was beginning to shiver, but I stayed in the water to watch her get out. She walked confidently to the towel I had placed on the sand.

Her breasts were—no, I don't want to write about her body like that. She lay on her back, my towel beneath her, propped up on her elbows.

Naked. Watching me.

Oh God! It's only been a few hours since, and I already want to go back there. Have I ever been more alive than in that moment, ever full of more intense contradictory emotions, ever more aware of the present? I stood in the water up to my waist, hesitating. It had never been like this before. I'd never been watched with such confidence. The girls in my past were different. Compared to V, they had no meaning.

"What are you waiting for?" she said. I thought I heard a slight crack in her voice, a barely decipherable hint of nerves. "Make me warm again."

That was enough for me. I left the water and lay down beside her, and then—

I won't describe it. In my other diaries, I've written about the girls I've been with, the details of their bodies, what we did to each other, how they felt, the noises they made—all of it. But it's cheap and I won't do it to her.

Just now, I dropped my pen and replayed it in my mind. It can't be the last time. It won't be. I won't let it.

Afterward, I began to talk. I told her more than I should —not just about myself, but about my mother and her addictions. I tried to get her to talk about her marriage, but she dodged my questions, and I soon gave up. She wanted me—that's all I needed to know. After some time lying in the sun, I tried to kiss her again, but she fended me off.

"That's enough," she said. "I have to get home before dark."

"We have time," I said.

"Oh my God, you're such a boy. But we can't be seen together. I need to be home early, dummy."

I touched her again, but she fended me off and dressed.

"No. If he finds out, he'll kill us both." I must have looked incredulous because she touched my arm and shook her head. "I mean it. I know he looks harmless. But he's proud and jealous."

"I'm not scared of him," I said.

I was surprised to see the concern in her eyes. "You should be. For both our sakes."

30

VIRGINIA

W hen I walk into the lawyer's office, she has the agreement printed out, with a few dozen Post-it notes marking pages of interest.

"Have a seat, Mrs. Eastman. My name is Patricia Ward. We spoke on the phone."

The conference room is completely bare, with a small glass table and bright fluorescent lights. The lawyer looks like she's twenty, but her profile online made it sound like she's been practicing for years.

"You've been busy," I say.

"Yes. Your husband's lawyers were quite thorough. I wanted to ensure I understood the details before we met today."

The door to the conference room opens, and the elderly receptionist pokes her head through. "You want a coffee, hon?"

I'm thrown by the contrast between her tone and the lawyer's. "Yes, please."

"Cream?"

I nod, and the receptionist beams at me like I've made her day. As soon as the door shuts, Patricia crosses her legs and nods at me.

"Now, you've told me you want to leave Mr. Eastman. Tell me the full story."

"There's not much to tell," I say.

"I'm sorry to interrupt, Mrs. Eastman, but there's always a lot to tell when a marriage breaks up. I want to hear it all."

I tell her everything I can about our marriage to date, including the move to Montana and his attitude since he's arrived.

"Forgive me, but I was led to believe on the phone that there's something else, right? Based on what you've said, I'm not sure we'll get much from the settlement. The prenuptial agreement you signed... Did you read it, Mrs. Eastman?"

"No," I say quietly.

"You didn't read this before you signed it?" She sounds like she can hardly believe her ears, even though I can tell she already knows the answer.

"I didn't read the goddamn thing, okay?"

At that moment, the door opens, and the receptionist comes in with a steaming hot cup of coffee. I mouth a thank you and push it away.

"Okay, well, it's airtight. If you leave, you get nothing. That won't be literally true, but it might as well be. There's a chance we can rule that the agreement was unfair, but I'm not sure we'll get a judge to agree." She taps her pen against the page. "What are your goals here?"

"Just freedom." I tell her about my debts. "That's all I need. Not half or anything like that."

"Half a million? From what you've told me about your husband's estate, that shouldn't be a problem for him, even if he's hiding some of it offshore. But unless he's done anything to violate this agreement, we'll have a hard time here." She removes her glasses and taps the pile of papers with her pen. "This is serious. It's not just the agreement but the legal muscle he has behind him. We can't go into this fight without more evidence."

I stare into the coffee. She thinks I'm an idiot, that I had been naive to sign the prenup without reading, but the truth is it didn't matter at the time. Richard seemed like a ticket to a new life, so I took it, whatever the consequences.

"He's having an affair."

"Okay. You're sure? You have proof?"

I take out my phone and show her the video I took outside the woman's house. She watches it twice, then looks up at me. "I'm confused. What am I looking at?"

"That's her. That's the woman he's seeing."

"Virginia…"

She trails off, but I already know what she will tell me. I knew it before I came in. There's no magical way out, no subclause that will get me free of this marriage.

"Can you get me more than this? If we know for sure that he's having an affair, then we might be able to come to a negotiated settlement with this team."

"More?" I ask. "How?"

"Text messages. Phone calls. Photos of them together. More than this, anyway. Witnesses."

"You want me to spy on my husband?"

She puts her glasses back on and then stands up.

"Mrs. Eastman, as far as I'm concerned, he stopped being your husband as soon as you walked through that door. Give me more. We'll get you your freedom."

31

VIRGINIA

"Hold it."

I'm in a downward-facing dog, and my calves are on fire. I look down at my purple yoga mat against the dark hardwood floors of the Frostwood Historical Association—upstairs from a coffee shop—where they hold beginner's yoga.

It's my first time doing yoga in years, and I'm already regretting it. The truth is, I hate yoga, but there's no reformer Pilates in Frostwood, and I need to do something during the day.

There seems to be no one close to my age in the yoga class, either. But despite that, I'm still pretty much the worst here.

"Twenty more seconds, folks."

At the height of the stretch, I think about Gillian. Her plan.

"To finish, let's lie on our stomachs and stretch out our lower backs."

When the instructor says we're done, I smile at the ladies

next to me and collect my bag by the window. Outside, I can see the mountains, which are overwhelmingly white. I'm used to a bit of snow in New York, but the scale here is different.

"Beautiful, huh?"

I turn around and find Simone's friend, Elsa, standing behind me. The rest of the class has already gone.

"Sorry. I must have spaced out."

"It's okay. You never get used to it. I grew up here and am still in awe of the place."

"It's amazing," I say truthfully. I am in awe of it. I'm not sure it's beautiful, though—more like terrifying.

As I make to leave, she touches me on the arm.

"How do you find living in the Eastwood mansion?"

Surprised, I stop. "We're not living there yet. It's being renovated."

"Of course. I forgot. A lot of history to that place."

History? As far as I knew, the mansion had been built by Richard's grandfather and was only a few decades old. "I suppose." I pause, feeling slightly awkward. It's been a while since I've properly socialized with anyone, and I'm finding that my words are sticking in the back of my throat. "Do you know much about the ranch?"

"You could say that." She points to the exit. "Want to grab a coffee?"

I follow Elsa downstairs to the coffee shop, Java Junction. After getting our orders, we sit in two armchairs in the back, next to a wall of posters advertising guided tours into the glaciers—and one advertising a cultural experience with the local Native American tribe.

"Don't do that," she says, following my gaze. "Rachel's a total fraud."

"I wasn't..." I begin, before trailing off. "What do you mean?"

"I'm Native," she replies. "The woman who runs that is not even from here. She was raised in the suburbs of Connecticut, and then she discovered she was about 3% indigenous from one of those DNA apps. Next thing you know, she's teaching white people about my culture."

I don't know how to respond, so I nod and sip the terrible coffee. I think about mentioning the protest earlier, but I'm not sure it's a good idea to wade into politics with this woman.

"How do you know the Eastwood Estate?" I ask.

Elsa looks down into her coffee and frowns slightly. "PJ went to school with my mother. I was a kid when they lost their property in the eighties. It was a big story in town."

"Really? Why?"

She takes a sip and uncrosses her legs before answering. "I don't like to gossip."

I almost laugh, as it's clear that Elsa has invited me to coffee to do nothing but gossip. "It's fine. I can ask Richard. He already told me that PJ's dad lost the ranch. Something about the stock market."

"Well," she says, raising her eyebrow. "There's more to it than that. PJ's father killed himself not long after. The poor bastard. People say..." She pauses and looks into her coffee once more. I tap my index finger impatiently against my cup. This woman is trying to wring every ounce of suspense from her story. "People say Richard's grandfather pushed him into the market. He was an investment advisor—there were a million of them in those days. They got paid for trades, and they pushed a lot of bad ideas."

"Are they saying..." I begin, unsure of what I'm asking. I

don't even know who 'they' were. "Are they saying he did it on purpose?"

"Maybe at the time. He did end up with the ranch, after all." Elsa gives a grim smile. "But people stopped talking after what happened to Richard's father. PJ had a rough time, too. He had a few stints inside, mostly from bar fights. The dude is strong as shit and has a short fuse."

Just what I need, an armed man with a short fuse and a reason to want us gone. I make a mental note to tell Richard to get rid of PJ. I'll miss Casper, but I need to feel safe on our property.

"Honestly, I admire him. Even though it was our land first." She smiles again, though I can see that it's not a joke to her.

"Wait, you mentioned that something happened to Richard's father..."

"He didn't tell you?"

I can see the glee in Elsa's eyes. She can't wait to give me more depressing gossip.

"I know that he died a long time ago."

Suddenly, her phone rings. It's obnoxiously loud, and she raises her index finger as she stands up to answer it. She talks energetically, her right hand gesticulating, before hanging up in anger.

"I have to go," she says, picking up her bag. "Family emergency."

"Wait." I'm leaning forward, in the palm of her hand. "Tell me about his father."

"Well, he didn't just die." She pauses for dramatic effect. "He was murdered."

32

VIRGINIA

After Elsa leaves, I sit for a few minutes in the busy cafe, digesting the news. Richard's father was murdered—but what does that have to do with the mansion? Given the state of our marriage, I have a feeling that Richard won't tell me the whole story.

I need to find out for myself. I spend the next hour trying to find out about the murder online, but there's nothing. I figure the local papers don't have their archives online, and maybe a murder in northern Montana isn't enough to get coverage in the national press.

That leaves only one other way to find out the truth.

The local library sits proudly in an old stone building in the town center. When I go in, I find a gaggle of preschoolers sitting restlessly for story time, their parents—primarily mothers, though there is one dad—sitting behind them. Two are on their phones. One is hissing at her little boy to sit still.

Before I left New York, I fantasized about this being my new life in Montana. There are worse places to raise kids, and I wouldn't mind being a stay-at-home mom. So what if our marriage is built on lies and omissions? Can't we still have a happy family? Can't I still have a baby?

Stupid questions, foolish dreams.

The story ends, and it's like someone has kicked a wasp's nest. The kids scatter, some to their mothers, others to the shelves to begin pulling out books at random. One kid cries. Another tells a meandering story to the librarian, who is glancing at her watch.

I can't have a kid, I think. I am one of these kids. Foolish, selfish, unpredictable.

I go to the desk and ask a young man with a nose ring how to find old newspapers. He copies a guest password onto a scrap of paper and points me to the row of desktop computers.

"Let me know if you need help."

I do, I want to say. Help me! But his attention has already moved to a lady behind me carrying a pile of murder mysteries.

I take a computer at the end and start searching the online catalog. Richard's father died when he was eighteen, so I run a search for 'murder' and '2006.' There are hundreds of stories, many following the capture and trial of a man who murdered his family in late 2005. It isn't until the end of the year that I see the first report of the Eastwood murders. It's a front-page story, with a picture of the mansion taken with a zoom lens from the street. There's police tape around the scene, with half a dozen cars and an ambulance parked outside.

As I read the article, I discover that it wasn't just a murder, but a murder-suicide. Richard's father was killed by his second wife, who then killed herself.

I wonder what her motive was. Was he cheating? Or did

this woman, living in this isolated place, just wake up and feel the ground slipping away beneath her feet? I can see it. Reality shifts and distorts; unimaginable acts become simple and rational. She's trapped. She picks up the gun and decides this is the way to freedom and peace.

She shoots him and sees that nothing has changed. She's still the same. Life is still the same.

So she raises the gun to her head and fires.

I try to type additional queries, but my hands are shaking. I'm back there. Steve, standing over the body, his eyes cold. I'm screaming and screaming, until he covers my mouth with his hand.

We need to talk, he says. *Before the police arrive.*

I turn off the computer and stare at the black screen.

"What are you doing?"

I look down to see a small blond boy, rail-thin and clutching a toy train, staring at me quizzically. His t-shirt has a picture of a cartoon dog, and despite the weather, he's wearing shorts and sandals. I unexpectedly have an urge to snatch the boy up and adopt him.

"I was just reading a newspaper."

"What about?" Before I can invent an answer, he keeps talking. "I like reading about trains and treehouses. My little sister can't read anything yet; she's only two. We live at 43 Maple Street. Where do you live? How many children do you have?"

I look over his shoulder and see a trim blonde woman in yoga pants following an infant crawling slowly across the library carpet. She gives me an embarrassed smile, but I tell the boy I have to go before she can engage.

"Okey dokey, smokey," he says with a cackle. "See you later, alligator. Don't forget your toilet paper."

As I walk towards the door, I'm surprised to find tears in my eyes. It wasn't too long ago that I thought I'd be bringing my own children to the library in the morning. Pushing a stroller through the park and sipping a coffee. Feeding the ducks and walking our dog.

It's a hopeless fantasy. Instead, my husband has a second family, his sister wants me gone, and my psychotic ex is threatening me.

My biggest hope is a clean slate. No debts, no husband, no ex—just a chance to start again. Maybe then, I can find someone new, someone simple and kind whom I can build a life with. Right now, it seems impossible—and maybe it always will be impossible. Because there's one thing I can't escape, the one constant throughout my life: The knowledge of what I've done.

Steve might be dangerous, but he wasn't alone that night. There's a reason why he thinks we're soulmates, after all. We're both broken in the same way. We're both carrying the same scars and the same history.

In the pharmacy, I ask about the prescription they ordered from Missoula and wait. After a few minutes, I'm given the bill. It's two grand, but it should keep me going for another few months.

I give the pharmacist my card and tap my fingers on the counter.

"I'm sorry," she says. "Your card has declined."

"No," I say. I should have at least double what I need. "That's not possible. Can you try again?"

She inserts the card and then hands over the receipt, which has 'DECLINED' in capitals printed across the top.

"Just a second," I say, pulling up the banking app on my phone. Shit—my account is nearly empty. I click through and see that Richard stopped payments to my account not long after moving to Frostwood.

"Excuse me."

There's someone behind me, so I move aside. I feel numb, then angry. What the hell is he playing at? I need to confront him, but it won't be easy. How am I going to explain how much I need the money?

33

VIRGINIA

I bike home in the dark, feeling uneasy as the traffic screams past me. Richard's right—this isn't a big city, and it wouldn't take much for a pickup going 70 to knock me into the ditch.

Back at the Eastwood Estate, I park my bike in the garage and walk to the field behind the house. The moon is out, and I can see PJ carrying a bucket down the hill. I figure it's to clean up more graffiti, but I don't care to find out. After what Simone told me, I don't want anything to do with PJ if I can help it.

As I turn to go back to the house, I hear footsteps sprinting towards me. I jump in shock—but it's just Casper. She leaps up and places her paws on my chest. I let her lick my face and scratch her torso. I don't want to let her leave, but PJ yells angrily at the dog and then lets loose a piercing whistle. I wish that I could take Casper home with me. I'd trade half the estate for her, maybe more.

As I return to the house, I see Richard standing in the

kitchen. It's early for him—he must have gotten tired of his second family. I'm even more surprised to see Gillian standing in the same room. She has a familiar smirk while Richard is saying something with great intensity. I see him slam his fist into the cupboard.

I'm shocked—I've never seen Richard so angry—but I'm happy, too. Maybe he's finally standing up for me. Or for himself, for that matter.

I go closer to the window, edging to the side so I'm not standing in the light. The window is a fraction open—Richard likes to let out cooking smells—so I can make out what they are saying.

"When?" he asks.

"Before winter," she says. It sounds like she's mocking him.

"I can't possibly. We can come up with another way."

"The way I see it, you don't have any options."

Suddenly, the wind picks up, and I can't make out what Richard says next. I step closer, but my foot settles on the gravel path and makes a noise. Gillian glances outside, but I doubt she can see anything but her reflection in the window.

She says something, and I see Richard constraining his anger as she saunters out of view. He stands there for a while after she leaves, staring at the cupboard that he's smashed his fist into.

I try to make sense of what I hear. Gillian is demanding something that Richard doesn't want to give—money, probably. A few weeks ago, I would have just asked Richard to tell me what she wants. But now, I don't trust him to tell me the truth about anything.

My marriage is over. Except that it can't be over.

I jump back as the front door opens and Richard storms out. He's in his winter running gear with a headlamp. I freeze, but he doesn't come in my direction.

The real question, I think, as I stand in the cold watching the bobbing light disappear into the night, is how long before he leaves me for this other woman?

34

VIRGINIA

That night, we lie awake. He's perfectly still, but his breathing is shallow and uneven. I calculate that we've had sex four times in the last six months.

How many times has he slept with other women? For all I know, he's been having affairs the entire time. He worked late practically every night in New York—he had plenty of opportunity. But for that to be true, he would have to be more than just a liar. He would have to be a complete and utter sociopath. Because the man I've known for all these years isn't the type to sleep around. He didn't have that reputation at work, either.

I think I know his entire romantic history, but what if I don't? How do I know anything except what he's told me? It makes my head spin.

"I had a conversation with someone in town today," I say quietly.

He grunts. "I was asleep."

Another lie.

"She told me about your parents."

He turns over on his back. I can see his eyes shining in the moonlight. "What about them?"

"Richard, he was murdered."

I feel his body stiffen. "Just my dad. She killed herself. And not Mom, obviously."

"In the mansion," I say. "Where we're going to live."

"Can you stop calling it that? It's just a house."

"Why didn't you tell me?"

He pulls at the sheets in agitation. "You wanted me to tell you how my father was murdered? I don't like to dwell on it. It's in the past."

"This is going to be my home," I say, propping myself on my elbow. I'm aware I'm on shaky ground, but with all his lies, I'm feeling reckless. "I had to find out from some random woman—"

"Don't listen to them."

"Who am I supposed to listen to? You don't tell me anything!"

"What does that mean?" He grunts again when I don't reply and turns onto his side. "Jesus, Virginia. They're dead, okay? You want me to give you the details about their grisly murder? What's wrong with you?"

Good question, I think to myself. But one for another day. He pulls at the sheets once more, then flings them off his body and storms out of the room. When he returns a few moments later, I get up. I can't sleep in the same bed as this man anymore. I feel the walls closing in, pressing at me, squashing me. I want to scream.

I go outside and stand in the dark. I look out to the mansion, that ungainly black block against the hills, and have a strange premonition that it doesn't belong, that it's an alien presence on this land. Richard's father was murdered in that house—and now, I'm supposed to live there, no questions asked. I need to find out more.

I turn away from the house—and then jump back in shock. Below the mansion on the hillside is a figure watching me. But when the clouds move, and the moonlight shines through, there's no one there.

I tell myself it's nothing and walk around the side of the house to the living room. Inside, Gillian is asleep on the couch. On the television, a man and woman talk intimately in a hot tub. The man's body is smooth and hairless, his muscles round and inflated like balloons. He looks more like a plastic doll than a flesh and blood human.

I suddenly feel an overwhelming sense of pity for this poor girl. She grew up poor with an addict for a mother, who is now dead, and her only surviving relative is rich. Who can blame her for taking her one chance? Her methods are crude, but she doesn't know any better. She's just a child. Not blameless, but not wholly guilty, either. She's been thrown into a situation she didn't choose and is just scrambling around blindly, like the rest of us.

While I watch her sleep, I feel my phone vibrate. I click through absent-mindedly, then freeze. I'm suddenly aware that I'm outside after dark, alone, in a place I don't belong.

The message is short and familiar.

Leave, bitch.

I don't recognize the number. I glance back at Gillian. She's asleep, so it can't be her.

That means it must be Steve. He's trying to scare me. And because I know what he's capable of, it's working. Because there's a chance that he doesn't want me back at all.

He might want revenge.

35

JAMES

3 November

I t was just before midnight when I heard a stone on my window.

"James. James!" She whispered my name—but then shrieked when I opened the curtains. "Christ, let me in."

A minute later, we were kissing on my single mattress. I was tearing at her clothes, but just when I was about to reach inside her pants, she pulled away.

"I can't. He knows I've gone for a walk."

"I won't take long," I panted, only slightly ashamed at my desperation.

"Down, boy." She stood up and kissed me one last time. "Leave your window open. I'll come as soon as I can."

"Tomorrow?"

"I can't promise." There was a spark in her eye, something unsettled and dangerous. "Only when it's safe."

And then she was gone, before I could protest, before I

could seduce her, before I could do anything to control the situation.

4 November

I'm on my mattress with my window open, waiting for her.

It's two o'clock.

Now, three o'clock.

Now, four o'clock.

I may as well get up.

I can't sleep without touching her again. What would my life be like if she regretted what we did and never returned?

She's using me. I hate her. I love her. I need her.

5 November

Robert yelled at me twice today; Klaus, six times. I have no energy to fight back. I'm a zombie. I want to sleep, but when night comes, I realize I won't get any sleep again, not until I see her.

She arrived earlier than I thought, sliding through the open window.

"It's freezing in here," she said, immediately removing her top. "Warm me up again."

We lay awake afterward, whispering, but she didn't say much about her past. We dozed for a few hours and made love again just before dawn. We clung to each other as though we were starved.

"You better go," I told her as she started to fall asleep. "Robert will be here soon."

"Screw him."

"I'm a bit spent, actually."

She laughed. "Don Juan can't go another round?"

"Don't call me that," I complained. "It's not like I tricked you."

"No, it's not that," she replied, getting dressed.

"What is it, then?"

The question landed in the room with a thud, and I immediately regretted it. She kept dressing, and it wasn't until she was standing by the window that she responded.

"It's an escape," she said.

When she left, I was... what would the poets say? Bereft?

Not in control, anyway.

And as Robert told me at work, there was only a month and a half until Christmas.

I need to push forward with V. Make her see a future with me without scaring her away. It won't be easy. Despite everything, I'm still just a worthless laborer. She could cast me off without much effort. I don't know if I'm her first affair or her tenth.

To be honest, I don't know anything about her. She never mentions her family, and I don't know what she did for work before marrying Richard. I don't even know her maiden name.

But every day that passes brings me closer to the end.

And I'm terrified of the end.

36

VIRGINIA

When I make coffee this morning, I see Simone pushing a wheelbarrow full of mulch to the garden. I thought she was done for the winter, but it seems like tending the gardens near our house is a full-time job.

On a whim, I make a second cappuccino and take it out to her. I find her kneeling in the dirt, packing mulch around the roots of the rose bushes.

"Need a break?"

She looks up at me and lets out a sigh. "Shit, yes." As she stands, her knees audibly creak. "I'm too old for this. And before you ask, I'm not telling you my age."

I follow her to a wooden bench overlooking the garden.

"This is fancy," she says, taking a sip.

"I'm basically a pro," I say. "Maybe I can get a job at Java Junction."

"Your working days are over," she says, shaking her head. "You won't be me, that's for sure. Ruining my knees just to pay the bills."

"At least you're outside," I say. "I used to hate working in an office."

She snorts and then shakes her head again. "Yeah, because who doesn't want to be digging in the garden in 40 degrees out."

I inwardly curse my stupidity. Simone thinks I'm a spoilt brat from the city, and I'm not doing anything to change her mind. She takes another quick sip, and I can tell she's eager to get away from me.

"I saw Elsa the other day," I say.

Simone keeps her eyes fixed on the garden. "So she said."

"She told me something. About this place." I wait for her to take the bait, but she just nods. "She said Richard's father was murdered in the mansion. I did some research and found out that he was killed by his own wife."

PJ appears at the top of the hill and begins to stride towards us. That man is always lurking around. It's almost like he has sensors on the property, tracking whenever I leave the house. I try to remember to tell Richard to get rid of him, even though I know he'll never listen to me.

"You've been doing research, huh?"

"What was I supposed to do? Elsa didn't tell me much."

Simone leans to the side and spits out a thick wad of mucus. "She shouldn't have opened her fat mouth."

I hear the familiar bark of Casper, followed by PJ's impatient whistle.

"Please. I don't have anyone else to ask."

"Ask your husband. He knows more than me."

"He won't tell me."

"Well, there you go. It's not my story to tell." She lifts her cup halfway to her mouth and then tosses the remains into the grass. "Thanks for the coffee."

"Simone." As she stands, I reach out to grab her hand. "Please. I need something. This is going to be my home."

She snatches her hand away as though I'm radioactive. "Lady, I told you before. This is not your home. You are not going to be happy here." She pauses and glances up at the mansion looming in the distance, its multitude of broad windows like the eyes of an alien creature. "And I can't tell you anything about the murder because I don't know shit. But if I were you, I wouldn't want to live there. That house is spooky as shit. It should be demolished."

She trails off as PJ approaches. Casper comes up and licks her hand, then mine.

"Go back to New York, Virginia," she mutters, low enough that PJ can't hear.

"What are you ladies gabbing about?"

"Nothing," she says, not meeting his eyes. "I have to get back to work."

As she walks back to the wheelbarrow, PJ turns his attention to me. He's wearing a winter coat, but I can't help imagining the gun underneath.

"Bit cold to sit outside, isn't it?" he says.

I gather my cup and toss its remains into the grass. "You're out here."

He looks away from me to the retreating figure of Simone. "I'm different, aren't I? You're the lady of the manor."

"What do you want, PJ?"

My tone is sharp, and he glares at me. For a moment, I see a flash of anger. I'm reminded that this used to be his father's land. For all I knew, he spent his childhood here before it was wrenched away. Before Richard and I returned, he could have kept pretending it was all his.

"Nothing." He turns to leave. "Let's go, Casper. Let's leave the lady in peace."

As I watch him leave, I think about what Simone said. It was different this time. She wasn't just trying to be rude.

She was trying to warn me.

37

VIRGINIA

After breakfast, I think about going for a run, but Simone has me too spooked to go on the trails on my own. Instead, I bike into town with my laptop and spend the day hopping between coffee shops and diners, attempting to plan my new life.

My new life away from Richard.

I still don't know if I can leave him, but it's worth having a backup plan. The problem is that the only backup plan is some version of my old life. When I met Richard, I was a communications associate who spent most of my time planning events and writing copy for the website. It was soulless, but when I graduated, it was the only job that paid enough to support me and pay down some of the interest on my loans.

As I browse job sites, I realize it's still the only job I'm remotely qualified for. I could try to break into a marketing role for more money or train to be a teacher and get less.

Here I am, pushing thirty, and nothing's changed.

I'll be a heavily indebted divorcee with no assets. Or a bankrupted divorcee with no assets.

I try to push these thoughts away as I make a spreadsheet of open roles and then refresh my CV. There's a significant gap in my work history, but it should still be enough to get a junior role somewhere.

By the time I get home, it's already dark. Gillian's in the living room, but it's mercifully quiet. I eat a lukewarm burger over the sink and go into my room to get changed out of my clothes, which are damp with sweat from the bike ride. As I lift my pillow to locate my pajama bottoms, I notice a lump in the bed. For some reason, I think Richard's got me a pet—a puppy, maybe, that's taking a nap under the covers.

I fling the covers across and then scream.

It's a head—a horse's head, covered in blood. I turn away and retch until I notice the smell.

It isn't the smell of blood and guts. It's tomato sauce. And the head is from a Halloween costume.

That stupid little girl.

I'm going to kill her.

"What do you want?" she says as I storm into the room.

I throw the ketchup-covered head at her, and she shrieks. "What is this?"

"You put that in my bed!"

She tosses it onto the floor, and it rolls to the wall, leaving a crimson smear on the carpet. There's ketchup on her hand, which she frowns at before wiping on the couch. "You've lost your mind."

This is too much. I feel like the contours of the room have lost their shape. Before the world can right itself, I find myself shoving her face against the back of the couch. She squirms awkwardly until I realize what I'm doing and let go.

This isn't me, I tell myself. *This has never been me.*

"What was that for?" she squeals. "I didn't do anything! I really didn't."

I step back, still shaken by what I'd done. "Who the hell did it, then?" She's about to answer when I hear the door open. "I don't want to hear it."

I go across the room and pick up the horse's head, then march to the kitchen, where Richard is taking off his suit jacket.

"Hi," he says. He looks pale, like he hasn't slept in days. "What's for dinner?"

I toss the horse's head onto the table, and he lets out a yell of surprise.

"What's this?"

"Gillian left it on our bed." He stares at it as if there's an explanation for what I just said hidden in the trails of sauce. "I suppose you're going to say this is all in my head as well?"

"Okay," he says after a moment of silence. "I'll talk to her."

"You know what this means? This is a death threat, Richard."

"Calm down," he says. "She's crossed a line. Leave it to me."

I go to the sink and take a glass of water. I can hear them talking quietly in the living room. She raises her voice once, and a few seconds later, Richard comes storming back.

"She said you hit her."

"Hardly..."

He's pacing back and forth, his shoulders hunched like he's carrying some intense burden.

"Virginia, you can't do that. She's a kid."

"She's far from—"

"Enough! This stops now!"

I stare at him, waiting to see what he will say next. There's a threat in his words, an ultimatum that remains unsaid for now.

He's thinking about leaving me.

No, I think, as I leave the room. *I won't let you. Not until I have everything I need.*

38

JAMES

8 November

"What are you doing with your life?"

I'm writing this by the moonlight streaming through the window she just climbed out of. It was different tonight. She came in half-crazed, snapping at every comment.

"What...?"

"Or what am I doing? That's the question. I'm ruining my marriage for a loser who doesn't even own a bed." She glared at me, checking if her blows landed. I tried to keep my face blank. Let her talk, I thought. Let this hurricane blow itself out. "I'm almost thirty! What happens if I leave him? Did you think of that? What am I supposed to do? Crash at your dorm when you go to college?"

"We can make it work."

"Please, you're a boy. What can you do for me? You have no money, no skills, nothing."

"Not for long."

She waved her hand dismissively. "You have no idea! Life isn't a video game. You don't know what it's like to imagine your entire future, everything, from every angle and see no way out. Ever! I have nothing of my own. It's all his, and he won't give me a penny if I leave. I'm stuck! Don't you see?"

The tirade continued for another few minutes before I gathered my courage and touched her.

To my surprise, she fell into my arms. But she soon turned away from me, her eyes wet.

I held her, not talking. Before this started, I had planned to act like a mysterious stranger and seduce this frustrated woman. I wanted to be a fantasy for her, someone not quite real. Someone who always said the right thing and made the right move.

She saw through all that, and I had become a real person. The problem is that my reality will never be enough for her.

"I don't think life's a video game," I whispered.

"I'm sorry. It's been a day."

"Tell me."

She turned to me and put her palm on my cheek. "Your eyes. That's why, you know. I saw those eyes, and I was helpless." She kissed me and then turned onto her back. "He's a cheat. He has been for years, I'm sure of it. He says he works long hours, but I know better."

"Bastard."

"I know," she replied with a fake laugh. "I'm a hypocrite. But I never thought he was like that. I thought he was... de-sexed somehow. It's like he didn't have it in him all along. But I'm learning that he just didn't want me. It's like I thought I was walking on solid ground, and now the lights have come on, and I'm really walking on a tightrope above... God knows what. I don't want to find out."

I turned away from her so that she couldn't see my annoyance. Did he cheat? So what? All the better. The bigger the rift between them, the more she was mine.

But then I saw a bigger opportunity.

"Do you have proof?"

She shook her head and then began to kiss me. I could tell her heart wasn't in it but that she needed it to be like this —intense, passionate, all-consuming. The noises she made were fake, but it was enough for me.

And then, she said it—her final lie of the evening.

"I love you."

I said it back, even though I knew she didn't mean it. She couldn't love me. I was a body for her, a vessel to express her hatred for Mr. Eastman. This was a move, a plan, even if she hadn't yet admitted it to herself. She wanted to use me to escape him. I was her only hope, even if I was just a boy with no money or power.

"I'll get proof," I said before she left. "He doesn't know me. I can follow him."

She kissed me again, hard. "This is where I saw him going," she said, writing down an address. "He told me he was going on a hunting trip tomorrow night, but I know he's going there."

"I'll do it," I replied. "You can trust me."

39

JAMES

10 November

I stood inside the foyer of the mansion from dawn, watching the house. He left at 9 a.m., putting his rifle and bags into his pickup before driving out. It was early on a weekend, so there wasn't much other traffic on the road. I needed to be careful. If I followed too closely, he'd notice.

I waited a few minutes before driving to the address V had given me. His pickup was parked on the grass just inside the turnoff. Maybe it was too early to go to his lover's house. I continued until I saw him jogging along the side of the road a few miles outside Frostwood.

I wished I had a truck. I could end it here. I could even make it look like an accident. Accelerate and swerve to the right. Send him flying into someone's front yard.

I stopped at a park on the outskirts of Frostwood, waited for him to pass by, and then followed him on foot. By this point, he'd been running for nearly an hour. He turned twice and then entered a nondescript office block. I counted to one hundred, then approached the entrance and read the businesses listed outside.

They each had their own buzzer. Spotlight Enterprises. Accelerated Development. North Montana HeliTours.

Next to the fourth buzzer was a blank space. This must be where he worked. I wrote the address on my arm, then retreated to a Wendy's across the road. I went through three coffees and a burger before he came out, around 3 p.m., freshly showered. He was wearing a dark blue suit. I wondered if V had got it wrong. Maybe he really was working?

I followed him on foot across town to a reserve. There was a river. He walked along the trail for a few minutes before stopping at a bench. I crouched down and pretended to tie my shoes. And what was I doing out here? The man was clearly taking a break from work.

But just then, someone walked past me—a blonde woman wearing a short skirt over black tights. Eastman was looking the other way, and I watched as the blonde attempted to sneak up on him from behind the bench. Just as she was about to surprise him, he turned and made a loud noise.

She screamed and then laughed.

They embraced. Kissed.

I pulled out my phone and took a few photos before retreating deeper into the trees. I could barely see them, but that didn't matter—I just needed to know their destination. After a few minutes, they got up and strolled along the river. Now and then, they would stop and kiss again—not passionately, like me and V, but gently, like an old married couple.

At 5 p.m., they left the riverfront and walked back into

Frostwood. They were strolling, deep in conversation, so I kept a block behind them. They went across town until they reached an Italian restaurant and went inside.

The light had faded, and it was getting cold. I waited on the side of the street for a moment, indecisive. I could return to her and show her the photos I had taken—but they might not be enough for her. I had to finish what I'd started. The restaurant's front windows were tinted, and I figured they'd be there for at least an hour, maybe more, so I found a sports bar up the street.

As I pretended to watch a football game, I thought about her waiting for me. Was she in my bed right now, naked, counting down the hours? If I was successful and she did escape her marriage, would I be able to share a bed with her for the rest of my life?

Idiot! I told myself that she didn't love me, that she was using me, that I was just a poorly made raft she was clinging to, just to keep from drowning.

Did it matter? She was mine. That's what I wanted. I never needed her undying love.

Around seven, I returned to the Italian place and waited across the road in an alleyway between a bait shop and a dentist's office. It was dark, and the further down I went, the more pungent the smell of urine. I stood there for nearly an hour in the cold, watching the entrance to the restaurant, repeating my dumb fantasy.

Her warm body in my bed, every night, forever.

When they came out, I could tell they were both a little drunk. Her voice was loud, and his laugh was like the bark of a dog. While they stood arm-in-arm, I took another photo.

A taxi pulled up, and they got inside. After it drove away, I jogged back to my scooter. I knew it was stupid—what was

I hoping to see?—but I couldn't help it. I felt drawn to follow them, pulled along by some unspoken force.

The taxi stopped at a prominent three-story place in a large section—number 29.

The curtains were pulled on all the windows facing the street, and I had a terrible feeling it would stay like that all night. I sat in the grass, half-hidden by a juniper tree, and waited.

After a few minutes, the door opened, and a young woman—a teenager, maybe sixteen—stepped out onto the porch. A small child of two or three ran after her and clung to her knees. She swooped the kid up and hugged her before handing her to someone inside. She said a few words, smiling, then walked up the path to the street. I held my breath, praying that she wouldn't see me, but she went to a red Honda Civic the other way.

A babysitter. If this was the right house, then Mr. Eastman was having an affair with a woman with a kid. I stayed crouched in the grass for another hour, shivering. By this point, it was nearly ten. This was getting stupid—I'd get nothing but pneumonia from sitting in the grass as the temperature dropped below freezing.

But then the porch light came on. I shifted further behind the tree as the door opened, and Eastman and the woman came out, wine glasses in hand. They sat on the loveseat and talked softly to each other. Then he put down his glass and started kissing her. He was soon touching her breasts. I found myself repulsed by it. This disgusting man touching anyone made me want to vomit.

I took two photos before they went back inside, but I knew they wouldn't show much. I needed better proof.

So I reached into my bag and retrieved my balaclava.

40

JAMES

The steps up to the porch creaked. I looked down at their two empty wine glasses, one stained with red along the lip of the glass. It didn't matter if I made any noise. They'd be too busy to notice.

I tried the door and smiled. It was unlocked.

I stepped into a long, dark hallway lined with green wallpaper. A nightlight had been plugged into a wall socket at the end of the hall, so I figured it was near the kid's room. Her kid was young, so I figured the adults' bedroom would also be on the ground floor in case she got up at night.

To my left was a large living room with a gray corner couch facing a wide-screen TV attached to the wall. There were dozens of tiny toy animals on the ground—families of hedgehogs, squirrels, and cats, all wearing clothes. On a chair were three baby dolls with blankets over them, as if they'd been tucked into bed.

I was shocked to find tears welling in my eyes. What was happening to me? The smallest hint of a happy childhood, and I'm having a breakdown. I wiped them away and stepped down the hallway, wincing at the sound of creaking floorboards. The door to the next room was half open. There was a dim light inside, and I could hear white noise playing —the kid's bedroom.

The next door was shut, but no noise came from inside. I stood there for over a minute until I heard a low voice from the room across the hall. A sigh. And then a fierce moan.

The door was slightly ajar. I stepped across until I could see through the gap. It was dark, but I could make out his ass cheeks moving, her legs splayed out, her arms pulling at him, her fingernails scraping along his hairy back. A wave of nausea hit me as he whispered, "Oh, oh, oh," again and again. And then she cried out.

I didn't have much time, so I took my camera out and snapped a few pictures. It wasn't much, but at least I would have something to show her.

"Who are you?"

I stepped slowly away from the door. Standing behind me was the little kid I'd seen earlier, now wearing a onesie of a pink unicorn. As she rubbed her eyes, I began to walk backward towards the door.

"I'm a friend of your Mom's," I said, raising my finger to my lips. "I'm just leaving now."

She looked at me with curiosity for a second before her face began to scrunch up. I held up my hand and tried to silence her while I backed away even faster. Just as she exploded, I was through the front door and sprinting to my scooter.

I crouched behind it for a second, waiting for evidence that someone was chasing me. But there was nothing, so I ran down to the washing line and stuffed a pair of her underwear into my pocket.

Seconds later, I was on my scooter, speeding back to the estate as fast as possible.

As I drove, I avoided the questions dancing around my mind.

Like, what the hell were you doing?

Like, what possessed you to go into their house?

Like, have you lost your mind?

I didn't want to know the answers.

When I got back to my cold room, she wasn't there. My bed was empty.

As I write this now, my hands are still shaking. Is the end in sight? It has to be. At this rate, I'm not going to last till Christmas.

41

VIRGINIA

I tamp the coffee into the portafilter and click it into the machine. While my espresso dribbles out, I steam the oat milk until it's just right.

After the cappuccino is finished, I stare at it with satisfaction. The oat milk isn't fluffy enough, and the beans are a little old, but it's close. It's almost a shame to drink it.

I take my creation into the living room and sit on an armchair. I stare at my phone. Gillian is directly across from me. Her headphones are in, but I can see in my peripheral vision that she's stopped scrolling.

Now, it's time to wait.

She sits on that couch in the living room like she's leading a sit-in protest, scrolling through her phone and getting high fourteen hours a day. Sometimes, she plays music, though not as often as before. I can sense that she doesn't want to be doing this. And who can blame her? It must feel like torture to feel your mind and body gradually turn to mush. Richard paints her as sad and pathetic, but the girl I see is strong, angry, and cunning.

This isn't a cry for help. It's a ruse.

I need to find out why she's really here. She's threatening my life—but why? There's only one way to find out.

"What are you doing?" she asks without looking up from her phone.

"Just having my morning coffee."

She snorts. "Don't you have a hot yoga class to go to?"

I try not to smile. The girl is quick.

My coffee is over faster than I'd like. I stare into the empty cup and wonder... How did my life end up this way? A marriage without love. A life without commitments, but also without freedom. Anonymous threats.

I just want it to be over.

What's going to happen when Gillian leaves? I like to think it'll be easier. But it will also just be us: Crazy Virginia and lying Richard, my cheating shit of a husband. We're like a science experiment. There's a slight chance we'll create something beautiful and new. But the more likely outcome?

Violent combustion.

"Looks like you've finished your coffee."

I grip my cup so tight I worry it might crack.

"Can't I relax?"

"Looks like you do nothing but relax." She sniggers into her phone. "And keep your body tight so he doesn't divorce you for a younger model."

I take a breath and pretend to stare into my phone. She wouldn't be talking like this if she knew what I'd done all those years ago. She'd be running for the hills.

It takes nearly an hour for Gillian to leave the room. I was worried she might take the phone with her into the toilet, but I suppose even an addict needs a break. I hear the bathroom door close and count to ten before jumping up and grabbing it from the coffee table, where she's left it face down.

I cross my fingers as I enter the passcode I have memorized

147. 258.

Like magic, the phone opens.

I almost drop it straight away. Because there he is—my other problem, right in the background to her phone. He's smiling at the camera while Gillian kisses his cheek.

Steve.

What the hell? My hand shakes as I open her messaging app. Steve is the first contact. I click it open and feel like dropping the phone a second time.

The first message is a picture of Steve's junk—close-up and aroused. I scroll down and find explicit pictures of her, too, taken in the bathroom or her bedroom late at night. Most of the messages are short declarations of love and desire.

> I can't wait to be with you.

> Not long now.

> We just have to be patient.

> It's going to work, trust me! It'll set you up for life!

I keep scrolling and find that the messages go back to just before my arrival in Montana. He must have found out my plans long before I arrived. I can't believe what a lying asshole he is. For the last four weeks, he's been declaring his undying love to me while sending pictures of his junk to this child.

> I can't wait to meet. You're my soul mate.

He's laid it on thick. More pictures, more messages of love. There are calls, too. It almost makes me feel sorry for Gillian. Whatever scam she's running on Richard, Steve is running one on her. And I know exactly what he wants.

Not money—but me. He wants Richard out of the picture so he can make sure I keep the vow I made before he went into prison.

Gillian writes in late September:

> Sorry you had to move out. It was a nice few days.

> I'll never forget it. We'll be together soon. Once we've finished the plan and she's gone.

> Don't talk about her!

Another text, soon after.

> Hmmm, I'm thinking about our first time.

I can't find anything about what they're planning. It doesn't seem like they've seen each other since I arrived in Montana. And how could they, when she barely leaves the house?

I click out of the thread and skim through her other texts. There are a bunch of other people—mostly young women, presumably friends from school—but further down, there's another person I recognize.

Richard, with his last text from just a week ago. I'm curious—since moving in, I'd never seen him say more than a sentence to Gillian.

"What the hell are you doing?"

Before I can open the thread, I drop the phone onto the couch. "I thought you got a text."

"So you thought you'd just read it?" She storms across the room and snatches up the phone. "My texts don't go to the screen, so you're shit out of luck. Christ, you're a stupid bitch."

Before I know what I'm doing, my hand travels to her face. She moves her head back just in time, and the slap is weak.

"What the..."

"What are you doing here?" My voice is unusually loud. "You're trying to scare me away! Richard doesn't see it, but I do!"

"You're crazy," she says, backing away.

I stay close, waving my finger in her face. "Yeah, I am. But I know what you're doing."

She stares back, utterly fearless. "You don't know shit, lady. And I don't care what you do. I'm not going anywhere."

I feel the urge to lash out, to throw things, to scream. I want to hurt this girl who was sleeping with my ex, sending him pictures of her tits while plotting how to ruin my life.

For a moment, I picture killing her—and that's enough to break the spell. I do what the doctors at rehab advised in times of high stress and leave the house without another word. I storm across the grass towards the mansion. Everything's somehow worse than I ever imagined, and I'm not handling it well.

I've smashed the coffee table, pushed her, and now I've slapped her. She's won. If she tells Richard, we'll fight, and if we fight, I'll tell him everything. There'll be no hope for us after that.

I can see the events unfolding like a Greek tragedy, terrible and unavoidable. My life's over.

Maybe I need to up my anxiety medication, but I can't afford it. And can any amount of medication fix the mess I'm in?

42

VIRGINIA

I storm across the grass, up towards the mansion. I don't know what I'm doing, but I need to get away from this place. The house, the town, the mountains—they're all pressing in. I can't think straight.

When I get to the mansion, I'm surprised to see Simone standing next to the old foreman, sharing a cigarette. When the man sees me, he nods and returns inside.

"What are you doing up here?" I ask.

She takes a final drag of her cigarette and then tosses it into the grass. It's been a decade since I've smoked, and the smell is disgustingly beautiful. It would be the easiest thing in the world to ask for a smoke. The only thing that gives me pause is how much Simone dislikes me.

"Planning the gardens around this place. It's a bit bleak at the moment—just grass. We're going to do something big. All flowers and plants native to the area."

I've never seen Simone so animated. "That sounds beautiful."

"Maybe... I don't know about beautiful. But it will belong."

The comment stings, but I no longer have the energy to be angry at Simone. She's right, anyway. I don't belong here.

"My ex is stalking me," I announce.

She looks at me like I've fired a gun. "Here?"

I nod, bouncing from one foot to another. Now that I've stopped moving, I'm beginning to freeze. "Yeah, from New York. He's an ex-con." I rub my hands together. "Sorry, I don't know why I'm telling you this. Not even Richard knows."

She raises an eyebrow. "For real?"

"He wouldn't understand."

"I hear that." She lets out a deep sigh, then takes out another cigarette. "What did he go in for?"

"Manslaughter. Ten years."

"Wow. That's a lot of time."

"He's lucky he didn't get more. He was breaking into someone's house. He was an addict looking for money. We... he thought the house was empty. But there was an old man there. He took a swing with a baseball bat, and Steve smashed a lamp over his head."

"Jesus. And that killed him?"

I look past Simone into the ground-floor window of the mansion. For all I know, someone is inside, listening to my story. "The guy was already at death's door. That's why he got manslaughter."

"And now he's stalking you, huh?"

"Before he went inside, I made some promises. I said I'd always be there for him. I'd visit him every week and write him letters. All of it."

"Pfft," she says and spits into the grass. "You were kids."

"No," I say, shaking my head. "It was real. I owe him."

"Bullshit." I watch her take a drag of her cigarette and exhale. "What are you going to do about it?"

"Follow your advice, I guess," I say quietly. "Leave."

She takes another drag, then stares at the cigarette before tossing it into the grass. "If some asshole is after you, there's only one thing to do. Get a weapon and scare him back. Get Mr. Eastman to give you some lessons—he's a hunter."

I'm surprised to see Simone this fired up.

"Thanks," I say.

"Don't get me wrong," she replies, stepping back towards the mansion's front door. "I still think you should get the hell out of here."

When the door closes, I take out my phone and call the lawyer. If it's a choice between leaving my marriage and shooting someone, the choice is clear. I'm not a cowboy, and I don't want to kill.

Not again.

43

JAMES

12 November

I left work early today to get to the library before it closed at six. Klaus got it into his head that I had a date and made crass remarks throughout the day. It was infuriating but better than getting yelled at.

Only twice did I imagine swinging my sledgehammer into the side of his head. Aren't I a saint?

I parked on the street and, for a moment, enjoyed the energy of the place. The work day was ending, and the streets were full of shoppers and tourists.

They looked happy, but I wondered how many of them were truly alive. Were they sleepwalking? Or were they awake to the actual intensity of life?

I sound like an idiot, don't I? Like a teenager. But I still am a teenager. But does that mean my thoughts and emotions aren't real? I don't think so.

She feels it, too. Doesn't she? Or is she lying? Am I being tricked?

No. It isn't possible. She feels it.

She loves me.

Stop!

Aside from a table of old women playing Scrabble, the library was mostly empty. I plugged my phone into the computer and sent my photos to the nearest printer. My phone camera was terrible, and the library printer wasn't much better. The photos came out like abstract paintings— but you could still see the truth if you knew what you were looking at.

I looked over my shoulder before checking that they had all been printed.

That was his hand. That was her mouth. That was his ass.

It would be enough for her.

I lie awake tonight, alone but excited for what this means.

I'm close.

14 November

She hasn't come yet, so I turned my attention to *Engineering Fundamentals*. I'm halfway through the textbook. Some of the math is more advanced than I'm used to, but the concepts are easy enough to understand. With this head start, I'll be at the top of the class when I go to college. The place I'm from, my high school, my mother, my accent— none of it will matter anymore.

I'll be the brilliant one. The special one.

After four years, I'll get an MEng from MIT and then an MBA from Harvard or Yale.

At twenty-eight, I'll be unstoppable.

I'll be able to reshape the earth. Level mountains, move rivers, build entirely new geographies. Cities will bloom, the fates of nations will change. I'll have tens of thousands of Roberts and Klauses punishing their bodies so that I can finish my projects on time.

If I tell her my ambition, will she laugh at me? She thinks I'm a poet. But I don't want to write beautiful lines about the world. I want to shape it in my image.

Christ, it sounds ridiculous when I read these words back. But aren't all ambitions absurd until suddenly, spectacularly, they are made real?

16 November

Something happened today. What can I call it? The last straw? The nail in my coffin?

Or is it more accurate to say that I've fallen? That's what we do. We fall in love; we fall into each other. Or do we fall into the void?

Here's what it is. I barely know how to describe it. She was on the edge of the bed, dressing, and I caught a glimpse of her slender naked back, her chestnut hair falling just past her shoulders. She looked back at me and smiled, and I didn't just see that she loved me, but I felt it, the desperate warmth of it. I wanted to keep her in that room, that bed, for the rest of the day, and after that day, the rest of the week, and after that week, a month, a year, a life.

A life!

When she came over, she was in a strange mood, more fearful than usual. We immediately made love. It had been nearly a week, and we were both starving for each other.

We're not like them, I thought. We're not like your seedy

husband and that stupid woman. They're just animals rutting in the barn. He's probably run through a hundred women like her, playing on their desperation for a better life, then leaving them sad, hopeless, used.

Afterward, she lay down and rested her head on my shoulder.

"Do you think he suspects anything?"

She shook her head. "He doesn't care enough to be suspicious."

"He isn't jealous?" I remembered what she told me about Mr. Eastman—that he was dangerous.

"If he knew about us, he would kill us. But he thinks he's broken me."

I stroked her hair slowly, and she raised her leg to my upper thigh. "Why would he want to break you?"

"That's what he does to people. He overwhelms them. It's why he's so good at business. He forces people to be who he wants them to be." She ran her index finger through my sparse chest hair. "I'm the silent, passive wife. But I'm losing my mind in that house."

I suddenly wanted to rescue her, to take her away from this terrible fate. "Leave him."

Her body tensed. "Don't be stupid."

"We could leave today."

She moved off me and propped her head up on her elbow. "How much money do you have in your bank account?"

"Huh?"

"How much? Right now."

"$1500." It was the total of what I'd been paid since coming on the estate, less the cost of food. I'd given all the money I'd earned at my high school jobs to my mother. "Okay, I get it."

"No, you don't. I have nothing. He controls everything. You think I'm a rich woman, but I'm not. I'm the kept woman of a rich man. If I leave, I get nothing."

"We'd be together." I paused. "I love you."

"And I love you. But I don't want that life. I need more."

What was I saying? I had offered to take her away from this place, but that wasn't what I wanted. That wasn't the plan. That wasn't why I'd come all this way.

I wanted to have her—but I had never wanted to love her.

Do I change course? Our time is running out. As soon as I leave my job on the estate, we'll be finished. What else could seriously happen? Will I find an apartment in town or a shack on a neighboring farm so we can continue our affair until he finds out? Which he will, eventually. Frostwood is just a town, and everyone knows the Eastman Estate. If V's right, he would kill us both.

Before she left, I gave her the photos. She looked at them for a full minute. I expected questions—like, how the hell did I get a photo of them in bed? But she was just quiet.

"Will they help?" I asked to break the silence. "Could you get a divorce?"

I saw tears in her eyes. She was scared of him—too scared, maybe, to do what needed to be done.

"I don't know, James."

I thought she would thank me like I was some kind of hero. I had practically risked my life, after all. But she just left without saying another word.

Now, I feel her absence. I want to spend the whole night with her, our bodies coiled together against the cold.

Let's put the question plainly. Does my love outweigh my hate? Eighteen years of poison. My blood runs thick with it. It's in every pore, every organ, every synapse of my brain.

I'm scared to think of what will happen next.

44

VIRGINIA

The lawyer set the appointment for 9 a.m., so as soon as Richard's gone, I make a quick breakfast and go out on the bike. I'm grateful it's a clear day, as I still don't have my own car or my own money.

But as I wheel my bike out of the garage, I notice a wire hanging off the side of the bike. I follow it to the back wheel and see that it's the brake line. It's been damaged. But how? This is a new bike, and I only take it on the road.

I look closer at the line and see that the edge is smooth. It hasn't been torn off—it's been cut.

While staring at the line, I notice that the back wheel is wobbling in an unusual way. I give it a rough shake, and one of the bolts holding the wheel to the frame falls off. I try some of the other bolts and see that they've been loosened, too.

I stay crouched on the driveway, staring at the bike. This is bigger than a prank. I can deal with salt in my coffee. I can deal with threats.

But this is more than that. If she'd been more subtle, I

might have been on the road with an aggressive driver giving me only a few inches of clearance.

I picture the wheel falling off, my body tumbling forward, and my head and torso getting pulled under the back wheels of a truck.

If she'd been a bit more subtle.

This is wishful thinking. I know immediately that this isn't Gillian—it's Steve. He's told her what to do, and she's screwed it up.

Which means he isn't just here to break up my marriage. He's here to make me pay.

As I go back inside, I call the lawyer and reschedule, then take the ring of spare keys next to the door. I know there's a key to unlock the garage and one for the mansion up on the hill. But there are also a few other keys, and I'm hoping one of them will do the job.

I wheel my bike into the garage and park it at the back, next to a large metal box.

Richard's gun safe.

I take out the keys and try them until the safe pops open.

There are three rifles and two handguns. At the bottom of the safe is a pile of ammunition. I don't know the first thing about guns, so I read the logo on the side of one of the handguns, and then search the internet for how-to videos.

An hour later, I know how to load and shoot a handgun.

I place it in my bag with a couple of boxes of ammunition. Richard will notice they're gone next time he goes hunting, but I don't care anymore.

Simone was right. I need to be able to defend myself.

Or scare him away, once and for all.

45

VIRGINIA

For the next two nights, when I'm at home, I sleep in the spare bedroom next to Gillian's, with my bag—and the gun inside—on the pillow next to me. There's a lumpy double bed that must have come with the house, but it's better than sharing a bed with a stranger. I lie awake, searching for a way out. Anything that might allow me to get free.

But there's always nothing. I feel like I've been tied up with thick rope and am sinking slowly to the bottom of the ocean. The more I struggle, the more I hasten my descent.

Richard doesn't confront me. He avoids me altogether. He's gone when I get up, and I hear him coming home after midnight. I'd like to keep avoiding him forever, but I need money.

When I sleep, I see the murder.

They are in the mansion, sitting across from each other over a grand table. There is a servant, but he is dismissed. When the house is empty, they begin to scream at each other. She sweeps the dishes off the table and smashes everything in sight. He hits her. Then she has a gun. "Never again," she says, and kills him. Then she screams and kills herself.

In another dream, there is no fight. They sit calmly by an enormous fireplace, talking quietly. Then she pulls out a small revolver and tells Richard's father it's over. That she can't put up with his affairs any longer. He panics and says that he'll grant her a divorce, she'll get money, whatever she needs. But she just gives a pitying smile. Then she shoots. She watches him die before raising the gun to her temple.

The dreams merge with my memories so that sometimes it isn't Richard who dies but the old man in the apartment. In both dreams, I wake just as she pulls the trigger.

———

ON THE NIGHT my anxiety medications run out, there's a faint dusting of snow. I sit in my bedroom, waiting for him, rehearsing my lines, visualizing how I want the scene to play out. I need to be calm and rational. Richard has always responded more to reason than emotion. I know that if there's any hint of anger, he'll stop listening.

His car pulls in just after 11, his headlamps briefly filling my bedroom window like spotlights on a stage. The car door slams shut, and I hear his footsteps in the hall a moment later. He's heading to the kitchen.

I recite my lines again as I go to confront him. If everything goes according to plan, it should be an easy transaction.

But as soon as I see his blank, calculating stare, I know

how difficult it will be. If I thought I could resurrect any relationship with this man, I was kidding myself. We're dead—we've been dead for months, before we even came to Montana. Maybe Steve and Mom are right, and our relationship was never actually alive.

I don't love him. I don't like him. I don't even accept him as a neutral provider.

I hate him. I want to launch myself at him. Gouge out his eyes. Make him admit everything he's done.

"You're up late," he says, quickly looking away. He takes a knife from the cupboard and begins slicing bread.

This hatred is the only passion I've ever felt for this man, and it terrifies me.

"You too. Didn't you eat?"

My voice lacks the upbeat, casual tone I wanted. I don't know how to pretend anymore.

"Flat out. You know how it is."

I don't, though. I was never at his level. When I worked, I never really had any responsibility for anything. The receptionist probably outranked me. Work had always been more dull than stressful.

"Haven't seen you for a few days."

This isn't the script. I'm supposed to pretend that my mother is sick and can't afford her medical bills.

"I've been working. Like I said, it's busy." He butters his bread like it's committed a crime against him, then layers on thick gobs of peanut butter.

"Sorry to hear that."

My lines: *I need $500,000 to pay her medical bills, and I need to do it without her knowledge. Just move the money to my account, and I'll pay it off.*

Then, the divorce.

"You're in the spare room." He says this like it's a casual topic of conversation instead of what it really is: The beginning of the end. I stare at him, not trusting myself to speak, praying that he doesn't ask further questions. Not now. Not until I'm ready. But, as usual, my prayers go unanswered. "Why?"

"I just need some space."

He snorts with disbelief. "You have nothing but space."

"I need more."

Don't ask why, I silently beg. *Leave it alone.*

"What do you even do all day?"

I'm surprised by the level of scorn in his voice. I've rattled him by moving out of our bedroom. He probably didn't think I had it in me. "Go to yoga. Ride my bike."

"You can't do that here. It isn't New York. Some rancher will knock you over."

"I'm not scared," I say—another lie.

He picks up his sandwich, stares at it momentarily, then tosses it back on his plate. "I talked to PJ today. Someone's been vandalizing the mansion again. Don't take it personally. It's just kids."

"Bullshit," I say. "It's Gillian. You know it is."

"I know no such thing. Why on earth would she do that? Her mother's dead. She's an orphan. She's just in mourning—"

"You can't be this naive! Seriously."

"The girl is traumatized, Virginia. She's acting out, but she's just a kid."

"Yeah, I've heard that before. But she's not some innocent kid. And she wants me gone. She's making it pretty damn obvious. I don't know why." I took a breath, hoping it would stop me before I said anything I couldn't take back. But it doesn't work—all my anxieties and fears are coming out. "But I think you know why."

"What does that mean?" he snaps, his eyes flashing.

I've never seen him this angry. I hesitate—but I can't stop now. "I saw you arguing. I was outside."

"What did you hear?"

"Nothing," I protest, surprised by his question. "But you were pissed. So don't pretend she's just a traumatized kid. Something else is going on."

He picks up the bread knife and holds it loosely by his side before using it to chop his sandwich in two.

"I saw something interesting today when I was in town."

I'm thrown by the change in topic—and the sudden calmness of his tone.

"Yeah?"

"Someone called Steve. He was in the coffee shop, by the window. He even gave me a wave."

I feign surprise, but I know that I'm doing a poor job. "Really?"

"He said he was an ex-boyfriend of yours from New York. That he's been in prison but has just come out. He seemed surprised that I didn't know about him."

Shit. I had never told Richard about Steve because it would have led him closer to the truth. That I was an addict. That we had both broken into that apartment that night.

And the rest.

"Are you screwing him?"

Screwing. I almost laugh at Richard's inability to drop an eff bomb. "No. Definitely not."

"You don't seem surprised."

"He followed me here. He's stalking me. I'm scared—"

"So let me get the facts straight. Your ex-boyfriend followed us to Montana. You're free all day. We're not sleeping together—"

"Whose fault is that?" I interject.

He raises his hand. "And you claim to be doing yoga and riding your bike for, what? Sixteen hours per day?"

I'm surprised at the jealousy in his voice. I honestly wasn't sure that Richard would even care if I had an affair.

"Are you listening? He's stalking me, Richard. He's obsessed."

"Have you called the police? Have you reported this to anyone?"

"It's not that simple..."

"Why not?"

I couldn't tell him why I would never report Steve to the police. He knew my secret, and if he chose to reveal it, he could ruin my life forever.

"You're in love with him," he says, eventually. "You've never loved me, and now you're in love with your ex."

I want to tell him that it's not true, that I do love him, but that our love is different. With Steve, there were fireworks every moment of the day. Our love was chaotic and frightening. My love for Richard was always more steady and predictable—but that doesn't mean it wasn't love.

"You have no idea what he's done to me," I say. "You're blaming the victim."

He looks away from me and, bizarrely, takes a bite of his sandwich. When he's finished chewing, he looks at me again.

"I'm sorry. It's just, I love you."

"Bullshit." I didn't mean to say it. My thoughts are thick,

muddy. I can't control what comes out. "You're sleeping with someone."

"Nonsense. Why on earth would you think that?"

"You've been lying to me this whole time." *Stop,* I plead. *Don't do this. Not until you have the money.* But I plough ahead. The bonfire is lit. It's time to torch everything. "You're not working every night."

His cheeks fill with air, and he exhales slowly. "Correct," he replies, like I'm questioning him in a board meeting.

"I followed you. I saw where you went. Who is she? What's her name?"

"I'm not sleeping with anyone." He steps towards me. "Please, Virginia. Drop this."

"Do you have a daughter?"

He picks up a water glass and drains it. Then he laughs cruelly like he's mocking me. "Don't be stupid."

"You lied about your job. You lied about what we're doing in Montana. You're lying about Gillian, too. What else have you been lying about? What other secrets do you have?"

Before I know it, the water glass is flying through the air at my head. I duck out of the way just in time, and it smashes on the wall behind me. I freeze. I've been in this situation before, and it goes one of two ways. Either the violence ends, or it immediately gets a whole lot worse. I'm suddenly very aware of how many steps it is to the door, how large Richard is, and how thick the muscles in his arms and shoulders have become. How much damage this man could do to my face.

Just like my father did to my mother, again and again.

But Richard isn't my father. "I'm sorry," he says, his face showing remorse. I wait for him to say something else, such as explaining what he does all day. Maybe even, miraculously, the truth. But all he does is give a slight shake of his head and leave the room.

And with that, I see it all in flames. The bonfire grows. Our marriage is over.

Now, I think, the panic rising in my chest, *what choices do I have?*

46

JAMES

20 November

Today it snowed. The work site was cold, and Klaus spent the day swearing about the pain in his joints. Just before he left, Robert approached me and said that I wouldn't be able to sleep in the mansion much longer. They're installing new central heating, but it isn't functional yet, and the house will soon be freezing at night.

"It's a liability situation," he explained. "I can't be responsible for what happens. The pipes might freeze, and you won't even have running water."

"Give me a few weeks," I replied, caught off guard. I couldn't leave—I was so close.

"One week."

I stared at him and saw that there was no point arguing. I could make excuses to get a few more days, but it won't be long after that before I'll have to go.

21 November

I prayed for a break in the snow, but instead, it got even wilder. I can't leave my window open anymore, so instead, I wait for the sound of a finger tapping on the window. It doesn't come.

That's one more day over.

V! Come to me!

22 November

The snow continued until there was half a foot outside. I haven't left the mansion for forty-eight hours. I alternate between reading my engineering textbook and my book of poetry. Last night, I walked through the entire house at night. Twenty people could live here, at least. Maybe even thirty. But soon, it will just be the two of them. How will she not go insane?

The only way is to fill the house with children. Isn't that what a house like this is for? It's a monument to the power of a family. He probably wants to transform the Eastmans into a local dynasty. While she stays home, raising his children, he'll be out in the world, allocating capital and spreading his seed.

It's disgusting—enough about him.

V came again just after midnight. I heard the familiar rhythm of her knuckles against the glass. She climbed in and shook the snow from her jacket. I tried to undress her, but she shook her head.

"Not here. Bring the mattress."

I followed her up two flights of stairs to what would later become the master bedroom. Klaus had finished working on it last week, though it was still unfurnished. She walked over to the window and began to undress. Behind her, I could see the snow—and past that, the house where her husband slept.

I put the mattress down in the middle of the room and undressed also, watching her.

"I love your body," she said. "You know, at night, when I'm not here, I lie awake thinking about you. And I hate it. It was simple before. I was jealous of him, but I didn't know the truth. I had my life with him, and it wasn't perfect, but I could have made it work. Now, with you, the photos... James, you've demolished my house of straw."

I smiled at the strange turn of phrase. "What am I? The big bad wolf?"

"Yes," she said, her eyes squinting slightly as if confused. "You think I don't see who you really are? Honestly, I'm not worried about money if I leave him. I know you could do anything. Your brain, your ruthlessness, your courage..."

"What is it, then?" I asked, breathless. "Why won't you leave?"

She pulled me close and kissed me, then whispered in my ear. "Because you terrify me."

After we made love, those words felt heightened, almost ridiculous in their intensity. We talked easily about other things. She confessed that she wanted to be a writer, and I replied that I had known that from the moment I met her.

"Who else carries around a book of poems?"

"Am I that transparent?"

"No," I said after a pause. "You're endlessly surprising."

"It's only been a month," she replied. "The surprises will end one day, I promise you. And then what?"

It was a good question—but not one we needed to face. "I don't believe it."

"You're a child."

"When will you leave him?" I asked before she left. "I'm getting kicked out of here soon because of the weather. We don't have much time."

"Thanksgiving," she said. "I'll tell him then. I promise."

47

VIRGINIA

I'm lying in bed when I hear a knock at the door. I glance at the bag next to me and decide to leave it behind. Though I hate it, I'm suddenly aware of why people like PJ and Elsa carry guns everywhere they go.

Why wouldn't you if you could always be safe and ensure the safety of the people you love?

I open the door to find a man in a blue polo shirt with a clipboard.

"Delivery for Mrs. Eastman?"

I stare at the form. It's more complex than something from UPS, and it takes me a minute to notice the brand name.

Mercedes.

I sign it and follow him outside to where a brand new Mercedes SUV is parked near the garage.

"Enjoy," the man says, handing me a pair of keys and a folder full of documents. I tuck them under my arm and walk over to the car. The thing is enormous, with space for three rows of seats. There's a note tucked into the wind-screen wiper.

For our new family.

As I go back inside, I wonder when he asked them to write the note. When he ordered the car, before we even moved to Montana? Or after he threw a glass at my head? Is this an apology, or is it obsolete?

Either way, this is a start. The car is easily worth six figures. I could drive it back to New York and sell it. It would give me some breathing room with my debts.

But not yet. I still have work to do.

I walk past the hip-hop coming from the living room. It's been over a month since I moved in—I have to admire the girl's persistence. She's still occupying our house, making our daily lives just a little bit worse. She has to believe she's winning—in a small house like this, she must have heard me and Richard arguing.

I grind my beans in the kitchen and wonder what's happening to my thoughts. I can feel them shifting. I have a gun next to my bed—who does something like that? Not me. *I* would never do anything like that. I'm just a middle-class girl from Queens. I hate guns.

Am I changing? Or has my brain always been like a wild animal that is just now slipping its leash?

Tiger, tiger, burning bright.

It's a strange feeling to have no idea how you'll behave. To have a brain you don't control. To act against your best intentions.

As I labor over my coffee, I recite the rest of the William Blake poem. *In what distant deeps or skies burnt the fire of thine eyes?* William Blake went mad. That's how he understood the full sweep of life.

Innocence and experience. Yin and yang. Reason and violence. Sanity and insanity.

As I pour the frothed milk onto my cappuccino, I make the pattern of a love heart. I stare at it for a moment. It's beautiful, but as soon as I take a sip, it will be destroyed, just like all the beautiful things we love. We love the Mona Lisa, so we crowd around it till it degrades. We love the mountains, so we carve trails and campsites through the trees. We love animals, so we domesticate them, breeding the joyful wildness out of them.

We love people, too. And look at what we do to each other.

I sit at the kitchen table with my coffee on the chair nearest the door and wait.

It takes an hour for Gillian to go to the bathroom. The first time, I search the couch and coffee table, but can't see her phone anywhere. When I hear the toilet flush, I run back to the kitchen and wait for another chance.

I make a second coffee, then a third. I skim through social media and eventually open the video I'd taken of Richard's mistress. I pause on the kid and spread my fingers to zoom in. I wonder for a moment if Richard is her father. Richard often traveled for work. Maybe on some of those trips—when I thought he was in London or Tokyo—he was here in Frostwood, visiting his mistress. It wouldn't have been hard. I was never suspicious of Richard. Unlike Steve, he never flirted with the waitress or stared too long at someone walking past. I honestly didn't think he had it in him to cheat.

Is that the right word for what he's doing? Cheating?

Maybe it's worse than that. Maybe it isn't lust, but love—deep, permanent love. And what do we have compared to that?

I hear Gillian go to the bathroom again and sprint back into the living room. This time, I have better luck. She's left her phone on the coffee table. I quickly swipe in the code and go into her texts with Steve. There has to be a clue somewhere among the exchange of sweet nothings and explicit selfies.

She wrote last week:

> I can't wait to see you

> Soon. When this is all over.

I keep scrolling through the messages, until I find it. Bingo.

A pin dropped to a location deep in the Montana woods, followed by a message from Gillian.

> Stay here. Keep it safe until he makes a deal.

48

VIRGINIA

I find the location on my phone and leave the house while Gillian is still in the bathroom. It's fifty miles away, so I take the new Mercedes. I'm soon off the highway and onto long, isolated country roads, driving past nothing but cattle and empty paddocks.

After an hour, I turn onto a dirt road and have to slow down. I raise a cloud of dust behind me. The road ends at a muddy four-wheel-drive track leading into a thick forest. A "Private Property—No Entry" sign is nailed to a tree near the entrance, even though the map says it's a state forest.

I pull over to the side of the road. My Mercedes is unmissable, but I don't fancy taking the SUV into the dark forest. If Steve is out here, then I want to surprise him.

The trail is dark, shaded by enormous cedar trees, and I'm suddenly aware I'm alone. I check my phone but don't have a signal anymore; it's just the GPS. I wish Casper were with me. I smile at the thought of the dog barking and snarling at Steve.

I take the gun from my bag, tuck it into my waistband, and cover it with my top.

Steve's history of violence is longer than mine, if less dramatic. It started with regular outbursts when he was a child—first biting, then fist fights with other kids. When he got older, he started vandalizing property. He keyed his teacher's car, smashed windows in the school, and left graffiti around the neighborhood. He tried marijuana at twelve, lost his virginity at thirteen, and was quickly addicted to acid and cocaine.

Risk-taking behavior, they called it. A learning disorder. ADHD. Dyslexia. As the crimes grew more serious, so did the diagnoses. Oppositional Defiant Disorder was soon followed by Narcissistic Personality Disorder.

When I met him at the high school party, he'd just been released from the Bellinger Clinic after being diagnosed with Antisocial Personality Disorder. He didn't look like an antisocial person to me. Even though he was on a cocktail of drugs, he still had a spark in his eye—some hint of wild energy that I immediately found attractive.

"What did you do?" I asked when he told me where he'd been. I was just a high school kid from Queens, not very popular or rebellious. The idea that he'd been locked away in an institution was fascinating.

"Huh? He kept his eyes on the scene in front of us. Kids dancing. A couple on a chair across the room were making out. "I burnt down my parents' house. With them inside."

"Holy shit."

"They survived," he added quickly. "I didn't want to kill them. I think."

"Why'd you do it?"

He turned to me, frowning. "What the hell kind of question is that?"

I close my eyes, trying to block out the scene. Since I'd married Richard, I'd been trying to forget about Steve, the only reminder being the thick statements that came every month, coupled with occasional threats. That year of my life cost $500,000, and it was still growing. With my job in New York, it would take over seventy-five years to pay down. I was supposed to be grateful, too.

After all, my lawyers and the spell in rehab had kept me out of prison.

That, and Steve. He had kept me out of prison. Because of the story we had agreed on. The lie we had told.

I check the app and see I've accidentally walked past the coordinates, which are a few hundred feet off the trail. I backtrack and then spot an overgrown turnoff. It used to be big enough for a car, but without any maintenance, it's being reclaimed by the forest. After a few feet, I spot something on the ground that tells me I'm in the right place.

The butt of a cigarette.

Further down the trail, I count dozens more. I imagine Steve stuck out here alone, chain-smoking to pass the time.

The app says I'm close. I slow down, avoiding the sound of leaves or branches crunching under my feet. The trail goes for another hundred feet before turning into a clearing. I immediately step off the trail and crouch down low. There's an old caravan sitting in the dirt. Its tires are flat, and its dark green paint is flaking off. The curtains are shut, and there's no sign of life.

I recheck my phone and calculate how long it's been since I've seen another human being. I'm way out in rural

Montana. I didn't even see another car for the last twenty minutes of my drive.

No reception on my phone. No humans for miles.

A line from a horror movie comes to mind. *If you scream, no one will hear you.*

I quickly turn to look over my shoulder, half-expecting Steve to be standing behind me with a butcher's knife. But of course, there's no one there. I'm being an idiot. This is Steve. He's never even come close to hurting me. He's not here for revenge. He loved me. *Loves me.* For all I know, he's in Montana to break up my marriage and win me back.

I watch the caravan for another few minutes before deciding to move. If he's inside, he's asleep or watching TV. But the Steve I know wouldn't be staying here during the day at all. He was always a social animal. He's probably in a bar, watching football and using his crazy charm to make friends.

I stalk towards the caravan slowly, trying not to make a noise. When I get to the door, I touch the handle and turn it slowly. It's unlocked.

I go onto the first step and pull the door slowly—but as it swings open, it lets out a terrible creak. I'm so surprised that I let it go, causing it to slam shut. I jump away from the caravan in shock. If he's taking a nap, this definitely woke him up.

A full minute goes by, and I don't hear a noise from inside. He's not home, or he's passed out. Either way, I can take a look around.

Inside, the caravan feels even smaller than it looks. There are dishes in the sink and takeaway cartons on the floor. Two enormous plastic water containers on the bench.

I spot a cockroach moving towards a pile of fried rice

near the door. There's a large black bag on the caravan's only table, stuffed to overflowing with clothes.

Steve, what are you doing out here? You're out of prison, and this is the life you choose? I've only been here a few seconds, and I already feel claustrophobic. Imagine living here for a month in the woods where no one can see you.

It's dark with the curtains shut, so I flip the light switch— but then I realize it's worse out here than I thought. There's no generator, which means Steve doesn't even have electricity. And no plumbing, of course, and no way to empty the tanks, which means he's going to the bathroom in the woods or holding it until he can drive to town.

Whatever Gillian has promised him must be worth it.

I walk carefully to the sink and open the curtain to let in some light, then get to work. I start with his bag, going through his clothes and pockets. I open the cupboards, but there's nothing inside but cheap plastic plates and cups. I pull open the drawers under the bed, but there is still nothing.

It's worse than nothing because I don't even know what I'm looking for. I sit on the bed and think for a moment before going through everything in the room one more time.

Maybe he's in love with Gillian and wants to be close to her. Is that possible?

I stare at the wall until I realize I've left out one place in the caravan—a thin door off the kitchen. I get up and open it, prepared to be assaulted by a horrific smell. But instead, I see that I've found it. Why Steve is in Montana. Why Gillian sent him to this caravan in the middle of nowhere.

A safe.

49

VIRGINIA

The silver safe is sitting on the toilet seat. It's a little bigger than a microwave and completely out of place in this disgusting caravan. On its front is a digital screen with a numeric keypad. I press a button and see that it requires six numbers.

On impulse, I try Steve's birthday. 081987. He used it for everything—his phone, his computer, the lock on his bike. But it doesn't work.

Most likely, the safe will only give me a few tries before it locks me out for good, so I stop to think. What other numbers would Steve have chosen? On a brainwave, I'm about to enter my own birthday—Steve is obsessed with me, after all—when I realize I'm taking the wrong approach.

This isn't Steve's safe; it's Gillian's.

And I already know the code Gillian uses on her phone.

147258.

I try it, and it immediately unlocks. I open the door and see a black moleskin notebook, tattered around the edges. I take it out carefully. It's about two-thirds full of loopy handwriting. I start reading the first page when I hear the sound I've been dreading.

The creak of the front door to the caravan.

I close the safe door as quietly as possible and put the book in my back pocket. There's no way to escape—the caravan is too small, and Steve is too strong—so I announce my presence with a cough.

"What the hell?" he says, and a second later, the toilet door is flung open. "Virginia? What..." His eyes dart to the safe. "What are you doing here?"

"No," I say, trying to push past him. "What are you doing here? You followed me to Montana—"

"Don't flatter yourself." He backs away so I can leave the bathroom, but he's still blocking my path to the door.

"Yeah? It's a bit of a coincidence, isn't it?"

"Fine, you got me. I tracked you down." He suddenly reaches out and grabs my wrist. "But you made a promise to me."

I try to pull away, but his grip is tight. I see the ridges of veins running up his arm. When I knew him, these veins would be punctuated by minor wounds from the needles he would use.

"You're hurting me." I pull away again, and this time he lets me go. "We were children."

"I kept my end." He rolls his broad shoulders, and I realize how his body has changed since we were together. The skinny kid has been replaced by a gym rat. He probably spent the last decade lifting weights. "I gave up my life for you."

"What life?" I say, and he suddenly steps towards me, his fists raised like he's going to punch me. Instead, he swipes at the wall's light fixture, causing it to snap off.

"What life, you ungrateful little... You think because I was a junkie that my life didn't matter, don't you? You never loved me. You thought I was just a bit of fun, a bit of excitement before you went off to college? As soon as I confessed, you were jumping into bed with some frat boy." He taps his head frantically. "That's what I played in my head every night. But I could always tell myself that you weren't like that. Because you visited me every week. You wrote letters. You told me you loved me."

"I did!"

"Lies!" His fists are tight, and I wonder for a second if he's on meth or speed. He's twitching a little. "You just wanted to run. You thought that by leaving me, you could forget what you did. But I haven't forgotten. I can still remember you standing over that poor old man—"

"Stop!"

"You smashed his head in with the lamp, you psycho!" He let out a bitter laugh. "If anyone belonged in the can, it was you. I would never do that. We could have just pulled the phone from the wall and run. By the time the old man called for help, we would have been miles away. But you had to kill him!"

"Stop..." I'm crying now. My legs are weak, and the room is beginning to spin. "Please!"

"I can still remember the sound his head made as it cracked into the side of the table. I think he died then, don't you? There was so much blood." I fall to my knees and cover my face with my hands. "It made me sick, you know? Honestly, you scared me then. But I still loved you. And we all knew my record. I was going to prison or the goddamn madhouse either way. But you still had a chance at a real life.

You were just the innocent little girl, led astray by this big bad junkie."

"Stop," I whisper. "No more."

He kneels beside me, his face close to mine. "You don't get to give me instructions anymore. You owe me everything. You're going to help me."

"What do you want?" I say.

"What do you think I want? To hold your hand? To kiss you? To get you back? Get revenge?" He pauses and takes a breath. "I wanted to scare you, it's true. Maybe even break up your bullshit little marriage. But now I have something bigger on the go."

I sit up and look at him. His face is only a few inches from mine. The last time we were close like this was that night when we made our plans, a few feet away from the dead body. That was when I promised him everything if only he would give me a life.

Freedom.

"Richard?" I say.

He stands up and moves his arms like he's about to swing a baseball bat. "I can't get a job, Virginia. I have a criminal conviction. I can already see my future. Twelve-hour shifts in a warehouse. How long do I do that before I relapse? And how long then before I'm back in prison?"

"What is it?" I say. I'm standing now, wiping the tears from my face. "What could hurt him?"

He looks past me to the bathroom and shrugs. "She won't say."

My hand darts forward to push the door open, but he grabs my wrist and pushes me back.

"Now, now. What's the rush? You've visited me, so why

not stay for coffee?" He winks at me. "We can start where we left things. A last hurrah."

I feel the book falling from my back pocket, so I grab it.

"What's that?"

"Just poems," I say quickly. When Steve and I were together, I always carried a notebook to scribble down interesting phrases and lines for potential poems. Steve had no way of knowing that I stopped doing that when I married Richard.

"About me?"

"Yeah. About how I'm going to kill you." I pull out the gun and point it at him.

He laughs—that disarming, boyish laugh that always made me forget how dangerous he could be. "That's the Virginia I know. I thought you'd lost your spark."

"Just the dead weight."

"Ouch." He looks me up and down like I'm a new car. I can't believe he's ignoring the weapon in my hand. "I do miss you, though. We're meant to be together."

"Stay away from me. I mean it. I'll call the police."

"No, you won't call the police."

"I'll kill you then. Right now."

He shakes his head slowly. "No, you won't do that either."

He's right, too. I can't kill him, despite everything he's done with Gillian to hurt me. I drop my arm. "What then?"

"I told you. You're going to help me."

That's the problem with Steve: He knows everything about me. During our year together at Bellinger, I told him secrets I didn't tell my therapist.

Like how it felt when my father hit my mother. Like how her screams became normal. Like how I would hide under the bed and then hate myself for it afterward.

When Dad had his heart attack and died, it took months for the nightmares to stop. My mother's bruises healed, but life never became normal after that. Mom and I—we were broken.

"How?"

"Make his life hell. Threaten to leave him. Make it impossible to stay in Montana."

I think for a moment. "Why?"

"We want him to sell the ranch. It's worth millions, you know. Enough to set me and Gillian up for life."

"Okay." I say it plainly because I don't care if Steve gets his way. Richard will still be wealthy, and Steve is right; I owe him my life. "But I'm not scared of you."

"Bullshit." He steps towards me. He's wiggling his fingers like he's about to play the piano. I look at the prominent veins on his arms, an addict's veins pulsating with energy. I don't think he'll hurt me, but the gun is still in my hand. I'm ready to defend myself. "You love me. You know you love me. What we had... it was beautiful."

He reaches out to touch my face, so I push him in the chest as hard as I can. He takes a half-step back and smiles. I get it. Here's the proof. I am weak; he is strong.

But strength isn't everything.

"Let me go. You know what I'm capable of."

"We're both capable of a lot, baby. That's why we're good together. By the way, does the great Richard Eastman know what you're capable of?"

"Leave me alone."

"Don't test me." He steps closer to me. "Get me my money, and I'll leave you forever."

I push him away again. "Don't you want to know how I found you?"

"You followed me."

"Wrong," I say. "I got into her phone. I saw your texts. Your selfies. Some not entirely flattering photos of your penis."

He snorts with fake laughter, but his eyes are cold.

"You know she's a teenager?"

"I didn't do anything illegal."

"It's called grooming, dummy."

"She's eighteen."

"She looks like she's twelve." I'm trying to hurt him, and it's working. He looks furious, like he could kill me on the spot, but this time, when I push past him, he doesn't try to stop me.

"Get my money," he calls after me.

I'm soon outside, sprinting across the clearing and down the trail to my car. The world is shifting under me. The fall leaves are too bright, the mountains too high. I feel the swirl of life, too much life.

All too much.

But I know it will soon be over.

50

VIRGINIA

By the time I get home from the caravan with the book, it's after six. I had flicked through it in the car, but the cursive handwriting was difficult to read in the bad light. I could make out scraps of poems and references to a girlfriend. There was also a map scrawled in the back to a lake out in the mountains.

As I walk from the garage to the house, I shiver slightly. It's been unseasonably warm this fall, but it feels like the first dusting of snow at our altitude is coming soon. The hills are already white. Maybe when this is all over, I'll learn to snowboard.

You won't have any money, a voice inside replies, and I sigh. The argument with Steve had been weirdly clarifying. I keep telling myself I'm stuck, but I'm not. I can leave any time—divorce Richard, get a restraining order on Steve, go back to Mom until I'm back on my feet. I'll always be in debt, and I'll always be broken, but so what?

Maybe I could go back to school and become a teacher.

I unlock the door and pause. There's a weird sound

coming from inside. A repeated banging against the wall, coupled with the sound of grunting. It's unmistakable. Did Richard bring his mistress here? Surely not.

I step inside the house and shut the door as loudly as I can, but this seems to only make the noise louder. The grunting is joined by a ridiculous high-pitched moan.

This must be Gillian's latest gambit: To have performatively loud sex with someone and force us all to listen. If it is Gillian, then she's not with Steve. I left him at the caravan, and no one passed me on the road.

I walk down the hall and see it's worse than I thought. Gillian's room is empty. I walk to the bedroom I once shared with Richard and see a broad, muscular back and a clenched ass moving like pistons, covered by two groping hands. And under him was the soundtrack's source: A redhead with dark eyeliner.

She locks eyes with me and lets out another ridiculous, almost comically loud moan.

"Who the hell are you?" I yell from the doorway.

The guy lets out a cry of fright and rolls off.

"Keep going," she insists, but I can see the panic in his green eyes. And that's when I realize who the guy is—Adam, an apprentice working with the builders up at the mansion. I'd seen him around the property over the last month and had even been introduced to him on my tour when I moved in.

"Sorry, sorry..."

He stands up and covers himself awkwardly with a sheet. I can't help but admire his sculpted body. I even feel a little jealous. Why hadn't I started an affair with some hot boy?

"Sorry," he says again. "Please don't tell—"

"Get out!" I snap. I can smell the whiskey on his breath.

He awkwardly gathers his clothes from the ground and leaves the room. After I hear the front door close, I turn back to the woman.

"You too."

"Not without the rest of my cash," she says, pulling on some clothes.

"Cash?"

I'm pushed to one side as Gillian enters the room with a handful of bills. "Here you go. Nice work."

The woman stops dressing and counts the bills before stuffing them in the pocket of her jeans. "Pleasure doing business." She glances at me. "For the most part. It's a shame you interrupted. I was close. Honestly, I would've done that boy for free."

I glare at her while she finishes dressing. When she's gone, I turn to Gillian.

"I'm telling Richard." My voice is unsteady, but I try my best to sound assertive.

"Do your worst. Adam will lose his job, though," she says.

"Why the apprentice?" I remember the texts she had written to Steve. The professions of love. "Why didn't you just ask Steve?"

She shot me a look of confusion, then fear. "How do you—"

"He's playing you, Gillian. He loves me, not you. But watch out. He's unstable, and you don't know what he's capable of."

"Shut up!"

Within a second, she's in my face. I'm quickly reminded that this girl is as tough as nails. "You don't know shit about what this is. I feel sorry for you, actually. I'm actually going to meet him now. You'll see the truth."

Before I can respond, she's left the room. Not long after, the front door slams and I hear the sound of a car starting. My car—she has my keys. But I don't care anymore.

I sigh—and then laugh.

"I'm leaving," I say out loud as I strip the bed and open the windows. The air is cold but clarifying. "I'm leaving you all for good."

I pour a glass of wine, then go to the empty living room, lie on the couch, open the diary, and read.

It starts on the 12th of October.

51

JAMES

26 November

I t's the day before Thanksgiving. I watched Eastman leave at dawn, then crept down through the snow to their house.

As I descended the hill, I looked at the white mountains in the distance. The town would be full of skiers and tourists here to explore the glaciers. I wondered if my life would ever be that simple and carefree. I'd never taken a vacation in my life. I didn't want to, either. I won't work my ass off to sit in some expensive mountain lodge and drink hot chocolates.

Is it even accurate to say that these people are alive? Compared to me, they're just lumps of clay, waiting to be shaped and reshaped by the will of other people.

By my will, one day soon.

I opened the front door and found myself in a cramped hallway. After the high ceilings of the mansion, the house seemed claustrophobic. How could she have lived here with him all these weeks?

I crept past two closed doors to the bedroom at the end. She was asleep in a king bed, snoring softly. I took a half step forward, and a floorboard creaked, causing her to sit up in alarm.

"It's you." She rubbed her eyes and yawned. "My God, what are you doing here?"

I walked in and closed the door behind me. "I saw him leave."

"He'll kill you."

"You keep saying that, and I'm still here." I crouched beside her and tried to kiss her. "He's gone. And I need you."

She pulled away. "Don't. My breath."

"I don't care."

She gave in on my second attempt. She pulled away the bed covers, but I shook my head. "Not here."

"This isn't his bed if that's the problem. I'm sleeping in the spare room."

"I know."

She let me lead her to the master bedroom. He'd left the window open, letting in the cold morning air. Still, I could smell him—pungent, nauseating. But I had to do it.

"You're scaring me again," she said, unbuttoning her pajamas. "That look..."

I stepped forward. To stop any further commentary, I kissed her. She pushed me back onto the bed, their marital bed, and took me inside of her. I imagined them sleeping here together, talking quietly, touching each other, making love... never again! I pushed her onto her back. She was mine! Not his—mine!

"I love you," she said as I finished, and I said it back.

As if this had anything to do with love.

"THIS IS JUST an ego trip for you? To have me in his bed?" She was sitting cross-legged, dressed once more in her pajamas.

"You didn't have to."

"No. I wanted to. It's just funny." She forced a smile. "A pissing competition."

"That's not it," I said, standing up and walking to the door. My mind was foggy, and I couldn't think of the right words. "Don't make this small."

She suddenly stood up and ran across to me. I felt her arms around my waist, her face pressed against my back. "I'm sorry. It isn't small, is it? It's everything."

"You really think that?"

"It's my life."

I stood on the threshold. "You'll tell him tomorrow."

"Yes," she replied. "Now, come to the kitchen."

Without answering, I followed her down the hall to that boxy room, where she made me a coffee with a French press.

"You lied about the cameras, didn't you?"

She cringed at the blunt question. "Yes. It seemed safer to keep you away." She stared at me, unflinching. "But I'm glad you came. I need to tell you something. Tomorrow, you need to sleep in town. I booked you a room at a hotel. You'll need to pay for it when you get there." She scribbled an address on the back of a grocery list. "I'll be there after I tell him. With all my things."

"Why can't we leave together?"

I could see that she was nervous as she pressed the coffee slowly and poured it into a mug with a picture of a collie on the side. "Milk?"

"No, V. Christ. What's happening?"

"Richard wants to have dinner with me in the big house. You guys have finished the main dining room. He's ordering in." She flashed a false smile. "I don't think it's wise that you stay in the building while we're there."

I gripped the side of the mug so hard I thought it might crack. "Don't go."

"James, this is perfect. It's the right time."

"You want to have a romantic dinner with him while I sit jerking off in a hotel somewhere?"

"That's optional," she said, looking at her feet.

I found myself standing. I lifted the cup violently, and the coffee sloshed over the side. She winced as if she thought I was about to throw it at her. I caught my breath and placed it back down on the table. "Shit, I'm sorry. I just can't stand you being with him."

She came behind me and massaged my shoulders until I sat back down. "It's over, darling. You've won."

"It doesn't feel like it."

I felt her lips on my neck, my cheek, and then I turned around, and she kissed me. "Between the acting of a dreadful thing and the first motion is like a hideous dream."

She maneuvered onto my lap and kissed me again.

"That's a weird thing to say," I whispered.

"It's Shakespeare. Julius Caesar."

"And how did that end again?"

She just smiled and shook her head. "Tomorrow."

"Tomorrow," I said, pretending to agree.

IT'S DARK NOW. She will have dinner here, in this house, with that man, while I wait in a hotel room.

I can already tell how it will go down. She'll tell him that she knows about his affairs and that she's going to leave. He'll be angry at first, but then he'll apologize. He'll switch on the charm—the same charm he used to win her over years ago, the charm he uses for all his lovers—and she'll begin to have second thoughts. He'll make promises about money, about leaving Montana, about starting a family.

And as he speaks, she'll weigh his offer against mine. With each fresh promise, the scale will go a little higher in the other direction. By the end, it won't even be close. She says she loves me, but it won't take much for me to be relegated to a crazy, regrettable fling.

How will she get rid of me? Will she come to see me and break it off? Or will she tell Robert to fire me? Or will she instruct the property manager to keep me away?

She might even sleep with him in their new bedroom as they rekindle their old passion.

It's not what she wants. But she'll trick herself because it's easier than the uncertain life we have promised each other.

She's a coward, and I can't trust her to do the right thing.

So I'll have to do it for her.

52

JAMES

27 November

I spend the day in the mansion alone, waiting for them. It's just me and my thoughts. My plans, if that's what we call them.

Yesterday, I told Richard and Klaus that I quit. Richard snapped his pencil and told me to leave. As I packed my bag, Klaus yelled at me about commitments and growing up. At the end of the day, I doubled back through the trails in the hills and stashed my bag inside the tree line before returning to the mansion. I'd left my bedroom window unlocked, but when I got inside, I saw they'd already removed my mattress.

No matter, though. I didn't need sleep. Not till this was all over.

One of the rooms downstairs had its floorboards ripped up, so I waited in there, directly under the stairs. Richard came just after six, followed shortly after by a delivery service. I couldn't hear much from my room, just the occasional creak of a floorboard.

After seven, she arrived. I heard her walk briskly down the hall to my room—our room—to check if I was really gone. Then she called out a hello and climbed the stairs.

I immediately detested the friendly tone between them, the undercurrent of happiness.

It could be different. But she had to come to a romantic dinner with him and let herself be seduced.

It was her fault.

After five minutes, I put on my gloves, crept back down the hall, and climbed out of my old bedroom window. Aside from the lights from the upper level, it was completely dark outside. I walked around the halo of light in the snow and went down to their house. I entered the garage and closed the door before turning on my torch. Red lights were shining from the vehicles inside. I went past them to a large cupboard in the far corner. Richard Eastman's gun locker. It was padlocked shut, but I found a hammer and used it to smash the locker open.

Inside, I saw a Remington 870 shotgun, a .308 Winchester for hunting, and a Glock 19. I picked up the Glock and loaded the magazine from a box of cartridges. It was heavy. I'd never held a handgun before.

It was her fault.

I went back up the hill to the mansion—the Eastman Estate. The name felt poisonous to me. What a pretentious asshole this man was. How clear it was that he needed to go.

I climbed in my old bedroom window and went to the stairs. They were supposed to be on the top floor but might have moved around. After the first flight, I paused but didn't hear anything. I went up the second flight slowly, pausing at every board that creaked, but there was still nothing.

When I got to the landing, I began to hear voices. Even

though the house was supposed to be empty, they were talking quietly. Is that the right word? Quietly—or *intimately*?

I went closer until I was just outside their door. I could hear him telling a story, something about business. When he finished, she laughed. It was too loud to be her real laugh. Did he know that?

How could I have known this man's wife better than he did? What kind of pathetic fool was this man?

She said something innocuous about the weather, and he laughed. They were both faking it. This marriage was over; anyone could see that. But they were still pretending.

Stop pretending, V! Tell him! It made me want to scream.

Another thought crossed my mind. My vanity had clouded my judgment. Maybe they had their secret language, something built up over years of marriage, something more subtle and profound than I could ever understand.

No—impossible! She was using him for money.

But if she could use him like that, could she not use me? I don't know; I can't ever know. If she was, this pale world is even more terrible than I could ever have known. What we had together was the only pure feeling of happiness in my life.

If that wasn't real, then who cares about the rest? Let's burn the world down. Let the bodies fall.

But no. I don't need to make it easy on myself. This isn't a crime of passion, though it will look like one. It isn't even revenge, though the bastard deserves everything he gets.

It's a rational, calculated act.

It didn't matter anymore. The hideous dream was over.

My entire life.

I stepped into the doorway and smiled.

"Hello, Richard."

53

JAMES

Richard Eastman dropped his glass of wine in shock, causing it to smash on the newly polished hardwood floors.

"Who are you?" he said, though I could tell he recognized me. I'd tried to avoid him for this last month, but that wouldn't help the glimmer of familiarity.

"James."

He frowned, parsing his brain for memories of that name. While he was thinking, I walked over to V and kissed her.

It was cruel, but I wanted him to know the truth before he died. I had taken his wife. I was going to take his money. Everything he had was going to be mine.

"How dare you!"

V tried to pull away, but I held her tight with my left arm while I pulled the gun out with my right.

"Now, now, Richard."

He raised his hands, panic in his eyes. I wasn't just a punk kid anymore—I was someone to be feared. But I didn't just want him to be scared of me. I wanted him to see the truth.

"Leave my wife alone."

"She's not your wife." He looked at V, confused. "Tell him."

"James, please. What are you doing here?"

"You know this man?"

I gripped her harder so that she cried out in pain. "Tell him!"

"Okay," she said, her voice shaking. "Richard, I'm leaving you."

"What are you talking about? For this kid?"

"We've been sleeping together for months."

He puffed out his chest, his face suddenly full of hatred. "You stupid slut. What have you done?"

I let V go and marched across the room. She let out a scream as I cracked him in the head with the Glock. It was a stupid move—if he knew how to fight, I could have easily lost the weapon. But the silly old man just fell to his knees.

"I'm bleeding!" He looked up at me, the hatred gone. "What do you want? Money? A job? You've already got my wife. I'll give you whatever you want. A million dollars. Wired to an offshore account. I can do it right now."

He kept babbling for another minute. I let it wash over me. Here was the most powerful man I had ever known, and he was on his knees, begging for mercy like an idiot. If only he knew how helpless it was. How helpless it had been ever since I got the job as the builder's apprentice. Then, the die was cast.

He had been a dead man walking ever since he set foot in Montana.

"James, there has to be another way," V cried. "We can go

to another country. One without extradition. Take his money. Let him live."

I looked at her in horror. Was she begging for his life? I was suddenly overwhelmed with nausea.

It was her fault.

"No."

I raised the gun at this pathetic man, this colossus, this wolf. He had ruined lives, including my own. I couldn't let him live. V was a complication. I didn't want to love her. It made it harder. It muddied my thinking. I only wanted to humiliate him, transform him into a ridiculous cuckold, then end his life.

"You don't want to," she said, clutching my arm, weeping. I was weeping, too; I could feel it, my vision clouding till I could barely see the man in front of me.

"Enough," I said, turning to V and kissing her on the mouth. "I love you. But this is the only way. He dies, and you can inherit everything."

"It's not," she said, looking into my eyes. I saw then that she truly loved me. That it wasn't a trick. That she wasn't using me. It was real. "James, watch out!"

I turned to find Richard Eastman charging at me like a wild animal, his face bloody and cruel, and so I fired. The bullet hit him in the forehead. He fell down and slid across the floor, stopping just a few feet from where I stood.

I knelt and stared at the dead man. I want to say that it all changed, that all the suffering fell away, that I was a new man—but none of that was true. He was, simply, dead. And I was alive.

That was enough.

My attention turned to V, who I suddenly realized was screaming. It was powerful, plaintive, as if she were screaming not about the murder but about the world itself that led us to this point. How long had that been happening?

Oh well. It didn't matter. It had started. Now, it had to end.

Before she could gather her senses, I took her hand and placed it around the gun.

"Let's do it together," I said.

"No!"

Before she could pull her hand away, we fired twice into his chest. She then fell onto the floor, sobbing quietly. After a minute, she looked up at me, her eyes full of disgust.

"No. No. What have you done? No! No! No!"

It was a hateful performance. She regretted it—truly. I could see then that she wasn't the woman I had fallen in love with. This pathetic figure was just a spoiled housewife who had taken me as a lover to alleviate her boredom. She was playing out a fantasy. And now it was real, and she regretted everything.

I hated her, then. I took her by the hand and lifted her. She fell against me, gripping my arms so tight she left dark bruises.

It hardly mattered. I took the underwear I had taken from Eastman's lover and tossed it near his body. That should make the motive clear, even for the dipshit cops that lived around here.

I then placed the gun in her hand once more. She looked at me in confusion, just for a second, before I forced the barrel to her head and pulled the trigger.

54

VIRGINIA

I close the book and stare at the wall, trying to process everything I've read. It's the diary of a charming sociopath. I enter the date of Thanksgiving in my phone and see that it's from 2006. Just as I suspected—the year that Richard's parents were murdered.

This is a confession from the man who killed Richard's father and stepmother.

Does Richard know what's in this book? If he has any idea, then it's no wonder he's angry at Gillian. He could use it to reopen the case with the police. It could give him closure, once and for all.

Even though I have trouble trusting Richard, I want to help him with this. He's still my husband, after all.

His name was James. The diary suggests that he had a deep motive for killing Richard's father. James' plan from the beginning was to humiliate him. He wanted to take his wife, ruin his marriage, and then murder them both. In a moving twist, he fell in love—but that didn't change his actions at the end.

I lean back, staring at the diary, trying to keep the threads of the story in my head. What did it mean? Who was James?

After a minute, the diary drops from my hands. My heart begins to race. I don't want it to be true—but it's so obvious.

PJ. Short for Peter James.

Who did Richard's family hurt more in the world than PJ? His grandfather basically stole PJ's family land and caused his father to commit suicide. To get revenge, PJ pretended to be an apprentice and then put his plan into action. Later, when the dust had settled, he moved back and started managing the place on behalf of my husband.

It had all been fine until Richard moved back to the estate. Every day we're here, he's reminded that the land still wasn't his and that he's just a worker who can be replaced at any time.

I think about all the threatening messages I've been getting. I thought it was Steve and Gillian, but what if it wasn't always them? What if PJ had been responsible? It had been strange how the messages were still legible whenever I came across PJ cleaning them up—and how the culprit had never been found. PJ had always been the messenger.

What about the anonymous texts? They could easily have come from him.

It all makes perfect sense: his goal has been to intimidate us into leaving.

I take out my phone and call Richard. We haven't spoken since he threw the glass at my head, but it hardly matters anymore. I need to tell him everything before it's too late.

"Virginia?" he answers. "It's not a good time. Can I call you later?"

I clench my fist. "This is important. Are you alone?"

"If this is about the other night..." He sighs. "I'm sorry, okay? But can we talk about it later?"

"This isn't about that." I move to the kitchen window and look up at the mansion. It won't be long before it's finished. "Are you alone?"

"Hold on." He mutters something and then shuts a door. "What is it?"

"It's a long story."

"Virginia, please."

"I found something. A book. I think..." I pause, the words sitting in the back of my throat. What if I'm wrong? "I think it's a confession from whoever killed your dad. And your stepmother." He's silent for a moment. "Richard?"

"Where did you find it?"

"There's one more thing. I think it's PJ. I think he wrote it. I think—"

"Virginia! Take a breath. Slow down. Tell me everything."

I sit at the kitchen table and briefly summarize everything that happened, including my interaction with Steve.

"He's in the woods?"

"Yeah, way out."

"Text me the location. The state might be surprised to find someone living in the woods illegally."

"Richard—"

"Are you protecting him?"

I take the phone from my ear and hesitate for a second before sending Richard the location.

"Done." I open the book and run my fingers across the words. It seems impossible that someone like PJ wrote these sensitive, poetic words. He must be a true sociopath, the type who never shows their true self to the world. "You knew about the book, didn't you? That's why you're letting Gillian stay here and be such an asshole to everyone."

I hear him take a deep breath. "Correct. Someone anonymously mailed the diary to my mother. But she had already passed away, so Gillian ended up with it. She figured it was her chance to get rich."

"But why didn't you just pay her off?"

"Virginia, please, now is not the time. Do you have the diary?"

"Right here."

"Keep it safe, okay? That's extremely important. I'll be there soon."

I look out the window and almost drop my phone in shock.

"Shit."

"What is it? Gillian?"

"I think it's PJ. He's here now."

"Okay. Just be calm. He doesn't know what you know. And there's no reason to think he will do anything violent."

"What if he... Richard, I know that PJ's father killed himself after your family bought the land. It's him, I know it. And he's been to prison for assault. He's a violent person. And he has a gun!"

"Breathe!" Richard says. "None of that means he'll do anything right now. I'll be back as soon as I can."

Easy for you to say, I think, as he hangs up.

I just hope he's not too late.

55

JAMES

29 November

Did she love me?

I can still taste her—the salt of her sweat, her perfume. Her smile, the shape of her back as she dressed, her hunger for me.

I have no pictures, no text messages, no letters. Just this journal and my memories.

I'm sitting at a desk in a cheap motel near Missoula. I've used the money I saved on the job to trade my scooter for a cheap Mazda. I'll start driving home tomorrow, and it will all be over.

After the murders, I stayed in the woods for the night, watching the police and the ambulance survey the scene. I knew that if there was any suspicion that someone else was involved, they'd start a manhunt, and I'd be found.

But it never happened. In the morning, I circled through the property and retrieved my scooter from a sideroad, where I'd parked it the day before. When I arrived in

Missoula, I got the paper from the gas station and found the story on the front page. The journalist called it the Eastwood Murders. The police had already announced it as a murder-suicide.

There were photos of Richard and Victoria on their honeymoon in the Mediterranean. She was wearing a bikini on a yacht, and he was in a loose shirt. They looked happy, though I knew the truth. Victoria had settled for him and was never happy until she met me.

The journalist also speculated about the motives. The underwear was mentioned, and one of Richard's lovers was already being interviewed by police.

It had all worked exactly as planned.

And now, I have the rest of my life.

When I get home, I'll put this journal with the rest under the loose floorboard in my room. Later, I'll bury them in the garden. They'll be discovered a hundred years from now when someone digs the place up to build condos or a parking lot.

I'll be a historical artifact, a strange remnant of a dead world.

I'll never write again. The teenage angst that powered the other volumes, the self-pity that kept me writing into the night for years, is fading away.

If I ever picked up this pen again, there will only be one topic—one question.

Did she love me? Or did she just want an escape?

It would be easier to think that she was using me, just like I was using her. But I think that's not true. She saw everything I was, everything I will ever be, and she loved it all.

Who else will ever do that?

Stop! Enough! She will haunt me forever. But if I write about her, I'll go crazy.

This is the end.

56

VIRGINIA

Before I know it, Casper is outside, barking excitedly. Before I think about locking the front door, PJ is already there.

"Virginia," he says. "I have to talk to you."

"I'm just cooking dinner," I say, trying to fit the diary into the back pocket of my jeans. "Can it be later? Richard will be home soon."

Casper darts past PJ and licks my hand. I crouch down and scratch her behind the ears. She rubs against me, and I feel the urge to hug the poor animal and never let her go. I could do with a long break from humanity.

"Please. It won't take a minute." He hesitates before stepping inside. "Here, Casper."

Casper looks at him, but I instinctually wrap my arm around her enormous belly, stopping her from moving. It's only when PJ frowns at me that I loosen my grip, allowing Casper to trot back to his owner.

I stand up and face the man. He shot Richard Eastman senior in cold blood, murdered the woman he loved, then framed her and got away with it. He looks like a normal rancher—but I can't trust appearances anymore.

But I also can't give up without a fight.

"I said no." He looks startled at my tone, so I soften it a little. I don't want to give anything away. "Come back later. Please, PJ."

He looks like he wants to argue, but at that moment, Gillian storms into the hallway. "What are you dummies doing? You're letting all the heat out. Didn't you see the weather forecast? It's about to snow real bad."

"About time," PJ grunts before nodding at me. "I'll be back after dinner."

When he finally walks off into the dark, I lean my head against the door and let out a sigh. "Shit."

"What are you swearing about?" Gillian yells from the living room.

I ignore her and walk back to the kitchen. After a few steps, the poorly folded diary falls from my pocket to the ground with a slap. I pick it up quickly, suddenly realizing who I stole it from. I'm surprised Steve hasn't already told her what I did. Keeping my head down, I march into the kitchen and stuff it into the freezer behind the peas.

As I close the freezer door, I hear a scream.

"That absolute bastard." A second later, she's marching towards me. "Are you working with him?"

I feign ignorance. "Who? PJ?"

"Don't play dumb." She pushes me in the shoulder, causing me to take an involuntary step backward. "Have you been screwing him this whole time? Have you been playing me?"

She tries to push me away again, but this time, I catch

her arm and twist it around so she loses balance and slams against the kitchen table.

"Don't touch me again," I say, talking slowly. Gillian's young, but she's weak from the months she's spent lying on the couch. "If you're talking about Steve, I wouldn't go near him if you paid me. He's a stalker."

She stares at me for a moment before letting out a piercing scream. She leans against the fridge and then slides down to the floor.

"Chill," I say. "You're going to scare the neighbors."

She glares at me through the tears in her eyes. "You're loving this."

"What am I supposed to do? Have sympathy that he broke your heart, or whatever this is?"

"I don't give a shit about him." She screams again and slams her elbow against the refrigerator door. "It's what he has."

I can feel my phone buzzing in my pocket. It's an unknown number. It must be telemarketers, so I reject the call.

"He's a psycho," I say. "You're better off without him."

"He loves me."

"So? What does he have?"

"Something valuable of mine." She stands back up, looking thoughtful. "He says someone took it, but I know better. Maybe you can help me track him down."

"Not a chance."

"I'll leave for good. Give you anything you want. Money."

My phone buzzes again—a text.

Virginia, it's Simone. Can we talk? It's urgent.

I stare at the message for a moment, confused. How did Simone even get my number? And what could she possibly have to say that was urgent? It doesn't matter now. I have bigger fish to fry. I suddenly feel tired of playing with this girl. It's time to end it.

"I have the diary."

She stares at me, astonished. "What...? It was you?"

"I got into your phone and found the caravan. You should really choose different passwords—"

Before I can finish my sentence, she's on me, pulling at my hair. "I'll kill you! Give it to me! Give it, you bitch!"

I fall back painfully against a chair and tumble to the ground. She follows me, and as I cover my face with my arms, I yell, "It's too late."

"Bitch!"

"Richard already has it."

She stops hitting me. When I move my arms away from my eyes, I see she's looking away from me towards the door. Her voice is quiet. "Do you know what you've done?"

I take the chance to push her away and get on my feet. "Yeah. I got rid of you."

The blood has drained from her face. I wait for another angry comeback, but instead, she sprints to the front door and slams it behind her.

I close my eyes and let myself smile.

I've won.

57

VIRGINIA

When Richard comes home two hours later, I'm in the middle of packing my stuff into a suitcase. I keep expecting PJ to return, and when Richard makes a noise behind me, I scream.

"Hey, hey, it's me."

I feel the tension leave my body, and before I know it, I've collapsed into his arms. The last month feels like a bad dream. How did PJ put it in the diary?

A hideous dream.

I will leave Richard, but he's still the man I married and loved. I need to help him figure out the truth about his parents and help him get away from Steve and Gillian. After all, I'm the reason Steve got involved with Gillian in the first place. Who knows if she would have been able to torture us without Steve's involvement?

"Where is it?" His voice is low, even though the house is empty.

"What?"

"The diary."

"Ah." I go to the kitchen and take it from the freezer. "Sorry, it's a bit cold. Gillian turned up out of nowhere."

He grabs it from me and flicks through it before nodding. "Thank you. Did you read it?"

"It's about the death of your father," I say. "I'm so sorry. I don't know if you should look at it. Maybe we should give it to the police."

He stares at the book as if it were some sacred relic. "This has caused me a lot of headaches."

"I know."

He folds the book and puts it in a pocket inside his sports coat. "It's not over yet, though. Where is Gillian?"

"She ran."

"Where?"

"She just took off. She looked scared because I said you had the diary already."

"We need to find her."

"Why?" He's about to leave the kitchen when I grab him by the bicep. "Richard, don't you think you're burying the lede? It's PJ. The name in the diary is James. Peter James. His father killed himself. This is his family land. Forget about Gillian. We need to go to the police."

"PJ?" He looks confused. "Of course. But if he did it, we have all the evidence we need right here. What do you think we should do? Interrogate him? There's no rush."

A knock at the door.

I glance at him, then raise my eyebrows. "Worth a shot?"

A moment later, PJ is standing in the living room, looking agitated. I stay close to Richard—until I realize that Richard won't be any good against the gun PJ's carrying on his hip.

"I need to tell you something," he says, his eyes locked on

Richard. He's one of those guys, I think to myself. The type that only speaks to women if there isn't another man in the room.

"What is it?" Richard asks impatiently. "Not a good time, PJ."

"I just wanted to let you know I found out who the graffiti artist is."

It's you, I think, frowning.

"Who?" Richard asks. "Gillian?"

I feel a twinge of annoyance. Richard has spent the last month telling me I was crazy for thinking it could be Gillian. Now I see that he thought it was her all along.

"No, no," PJ says, looking surprised. "It was Simone Andrews. I caught her in the act trying to damage the big house."

"Why would she do it?" Richard asks.

"Her family has had some claim to this property for centuries."

"What are you talking about?"

"She's Native American. One of the local tribes. I mean, she's not wrong." He angles his head. "But water under the bridge at this point, right?"

I catch the irony in his voice. They had lost their land, just as PJ's father lost his.

"Want me to call the police?"

"No, no," Richard says quickly. "Let me deal with it."

"Are you sure? She's done a bit of damage, I can tell you."

"PJ. Let me deal with it."

"Alright then..."

Simone. I'm shocked. All those threatening messages— those text messages, too. She had my number, after all. Were they really all from her, not Steve, Gillian, or PJ?

"Hey," I say just as he's about to leave. "Did you go to college?"

He looks like he's about to spit on the ground. "You must have lost your damn mind."

"PJ," Richard says, his voice slightly raised.

"Apologies, Mrs. Eastman. I didn't finish tenth grade and barely went before that, either. My life's always been on the land."

I watch PJ walk out into the dark, then turn to Richard, who's staring at me, his brows knitted, as if he's trying to figure out some obscure crossword puzzle. "One second."

"Virginia!" he calls after me, his voice oddly plaintive. "We have to go."

I ignore him and jog across the driveway to where PJ is getting onto a motorbike. With Richard behind me, I'm suddenly full of confidence. There's no need to fear this man right now, and I can't go any longer without knowing the truth.

"What is it?" he snaps. "You want to know how many languages I speak? How much I know about Greek poetry or classical music?"

"Richard said you were single," I say, ignoring his tone. "Have you ever been in love with an older woman?"

He stares at me, his eyes full of hatred, then laughs coldly. "Lady, I've been nothing but hospitable to you."

"I appreciate it."

"I've worked this land for decades. Your husband..." He says the word with surprising venom. "He comes here after two decades and starts throwing his weight around, which is fine. It's his land. But I don't need to take these insults. Frankly—"

"What's the insult?" I say, interrupting him.

He looks at me with surprise. "I thought you knew."

"Know what?"

From behind me, I hear Richard calling out. "I'm getting the keys. Meet me at the car!"

He takes a deep breath and releases it slowly. "I'm not that inclined."

"You're gay." I think about the ferocity of the love affair described in the diary. Could someone have an affair like that and then come out as gay later on? It was possible, wasn't it? "What about when you were younger?"

"Christ, woman, despite what you might have learned in New York City, there are gay people out here, too. We're no different. And no, I never pretended to be otherwise." He pauses. "It's part of why I left school so young, if you must know."

"I'm sorry, it's just..." I stare at him, the truth slowly dawning on me. It can't be PJ. The boy in the diaries was summa cum laude and a Don Juan with women. It was also someone who didn't seem to know the first thing about ranching or the town of Frostwood, the place where PJ was born and raised.

"How long have you lived here?"

"Virginia!" Richard calls out.

"Sounds like you have to go," he says, spitting onto the snow-flaked grass.

"How long have you lived here?" I ask again.

"Forty years. Most of my life."

"Were you here for the murders?"

He looks away from me into the night. He brushes the snow from his face. "You found out about that?"

I hesitate before I say more. It could still be him. The boy in the book was also a practiced liar. Could PJ have spent his entire life here, faking his true identity? Or did he lie in the book to hide who he really was in case someone found it? But no, that couldn't be true. Those weren't the words of a high school dropout. Whoever wrote the diary was educated. And all the evidence said that wasn't PJ at eighteen.

"I found something. A book. It's a confession. I think it was by the person who committed the murders."

"Holy shit!" He stares at me before shaking his head. "What do you mean, murders? You're saying it wasn't a suicide?"

"That's right."

He keeps staring, then frowns and spits again. "You thought it was me?"

I decide to dodge the question. "It was the apprentice working at the mansion. You were here."

"I was young. We didn't manage the land then."

"But do you remember?"

"I'm sorry. I did some work on the house, though. Some odd jobs here and there. I probably met the guy. But it was a long time ago."

"This person had a motive," I say. "He wanted to kill Richard Eastman Senior. Do you know who that might've been?"

PJ looks past me, and I turn to find Richard approaching across the grass.

"I'm afraid I can't help you, miss," he says, tipping his hat and switching on his engine.

"What the hell was that?" Richard says as PJ drives off.

"Just asking about Simone," I say quickly. "She's a friend. Sort of. That was a shock."

He exhales in frustration. "We have to go."

"Let her go," I say. "It's over."

"You don't know Gillian." His voice is shaky, even emotional. "She's unstable. She has a history of self-harm. Now that she doesn't have anything over me, I'm worried about what she might do to herself."

I stare at him for a moment. This girl has tortured me for over a month and harassed him for even longer. But aside from me, Gillian is the only family Richard has left. He's trying to do the right thing, and I grudgingly admire it.

"Okay," I say. "I'll come."

58

VIRGINIA

We drive in silence in his truck. The snow has picked up, and if we drive for much longer, we'll need chains on the tires. As we pass through Frostwood, he makes a call—arranging for someone to meet us. Given the conditions, I want him to pull over, but I don't want to add another distraction.

"Who was that?" I ask after he hangs up.

"The chopper guy."

"Excuse me?"

He slams his hand into the horn and skids around a deer that has strayed into the road. I let out a scream, but instead of looking apologetic, Richard laughs. I wait for an explanation, but he immediately makes another call. He's apologizing to someone.

"Who's that?"

"No one."

"Richard!" I say, suddenly noticing how far we've gone. I had thought we would be going to the police station, but by this point, we're a few miles beyond the town. "Where are we going? She could be anywhere. We need to go to the police."

Instead of replying, he nods to his left. I read the sign.

The private airport.

"We're going to my cabin," he says as we pull in. The small terminal is dark, and only one other car is in the lot.

"In this weather?"

"She's there. I know it."

"How?"

He frowns at me, then swears under his breath before pulling out his phone. He presses a black, unbranded app on his home screen, and a map of northern Montana pops up— a green dot in the mountains about fifty miles west of Frostwood.

"You've been tracking her?"

"She's blackmailing me. I wanted to find out who else she was working with. It's only a tracker on her car with a GPS. We use them at work to track the fleet."

Blackmailing? Gillian had diaries that explained the death of his father—but was it really blackmail? I tell myself that it makes sense that he tracked her. He's a man of resources. It explains why she spent nearly all her time on the couch.

"How did she get there so fast?"

"Drove?" he says. "You can get there with chains. She had a decent head start."

"So why don't we drive?"

He slams his fist into the door. "Virginia, do you have to fight me on everything? I told you, she could hurt herself. She could kill herself, for all I know. We need to get there as fast as we can."

"I'm sorry," I say quickly, even though I think he's wrong.

The girl I saw didn't look depressed—she looked scared. Turning up in a chopper seems like the worst thing we could do.

Richard is acting strange, but I reason that it's hardly surprising given everything that's happened over the last few hours. He's close to finding out who killed his father, and he's trying to help the girl who has been blackmailing him. It's a heady mix.

I see a flash of light in my wing mirror, and a truck pulls up beside us. A short man with a gray beard gets out and frowns in our direction. Richard has a brief conversation with him before the guy shakes his head and hands him a set of keys.

Richard jogs back and gets inside.

"He's going to set it up for us."

We sit silently for a moment, and I try to smother all the questions crowding into my mind. Richard's father died eighteen years ago. Does that mean we'll never find out the killer? Did Richard ever investigate his death as a kid? From what I can tell, he still hasn't read the diary, even though that's the first thing I'd do. That must mean he had some idea of what's inside. Maybe Gillian had told him?

"I know this isn't the right time," I say. "But can I ask you something?"

Aside from a few security lights on the other side of the car park, we're sitting in the dark.

"Go nuts."

"Don't get mad."

He turns to me in the dark. He's smiling, but his eyes are cold. "Virginia, please."

I know I shouldn't, but I can't help myself. "The woman I saw you with. How long has that been going on?"

"What woman?"

"There's more than one?" I ask, feeling myself get angry. "You ran to her house one morning. She has a kid."

He stares at me for a moment, then laughs. "You thought I was sleeping with her?"

"You lied, Richard. You came here for her." I pause. "Didn't you?"

"Sort of."

I suddenly feel lightheaded. It was a mistake to ask the question, but it was an even bigger mistake to come here with him. I've been feeling unsettled ever since I saw Steve. Anything could happen.

"I need to go." As I unbuckle my seat belt, he touches my arm. "Don't touch me!"

"Let me explain! I wasn't sleeping with her. She's my sister. Half-sister, like Gillian, but on my Dad's side."

"Oh my God." I remember the scene in the diary where James follows the senior Richard Eastman to a house near the estate, just like I did with his son. James sees him having an affair, and he's interrupted by a preschooler. That little girl would be about the age of the woman I saw Richard with. "How long have you known about her?"

"Years. We keep in touch."

I want to ask more questions, but my phone vibrates in my jacket pocket. I see that's an unknown number. It must be Simone. I might as well deal with her while we wait, so I step out of the car.

"Hello?"

The connection is scratchy, and I can barely hear the voice on the other end of the line. It's like it's coming from another world. "Virginia... be careful... I won't see you again."

There are a lot of words in between that I miss, but the voice is unmistakable. "Gillian? I can't hear you."

She swears, and I hear a door slam in the background. "You don't know... James... Ruthless."

I try to stitch together the threads of what she's telling me. "Gillian, do you know who James is?"

"Be... name..."

For a few seconds, the connection is terrible, and I can't make out a single word. Then the connection miraculously clears, long enough for me to hear a single, terrible phrase. "Steve is dead."

I almost drop the phone.

"Gillian, what? Steve's dead? How?"

There's nothing but static.

"Gillian!"

As the call abruptly ends, I see a flashlight near the terminal. A man's voice. "Alright, folks. It's all yours."

A few seconds later, Richard is leading me across the tarmac. I feel like everything in my vision is a mirage, that we're all just characters in a game, waiting to be reprogrammed—or deleted.

Strange thoughts. Only Steve would understand them.

My Steve.

Dead.

Ten minutes ago, I would have said that I hated him. But I also know that I can't really blame him. He's imperfectly wired, a malfunctioning machine, and I drove him to the edge.

He's broken, and he saved my life. Is that all it takes for me to forgive him? Were all his hateful acts just aberrations from his true, gentle and innocent self? It can't be that easy. But I loved him still. I will always love him. Because of Steve, I got through the worst time in my life.

My attention shifts back to Richard as he helps me into the chopper. When he jumps into the pilot's seat, his jacket falls away, and I see that there's a handgun on his hip.

"Why the gun?"

He sweeps his jacket closed, covering up the weapon. "Just in case."

In case of what? I want to ask, but he immediately switches on the engine, and the chopper begins to roar. He taps a pair of headphones, and I put them on.

"She's dangerous," he says. It's like the voice is coming from inside my brain, and I realize there's a stubby mic at the end of the headphones. "Unpredictable. I'm not sure how she'll react when we get there. I want you to be safe."

I don't know what to say, so I nod. I see that he's right—we don't know Gillian. A person who can calmly bully us for months *does* seem like a person who is capable of violence. I realize then that I haven't brought the gun I stole from Richard's gun safe. I wonder if I'll come to regret it later.

"Steve's dead," I say, and he jumps in shock as if I've just shown him the body.

"How do you know that?"

"Gillian called me. She must have found his body."

We begin to rise. When we're safely in the air, he maneuvers south toward town. "Did she say who did it?"

It's an odd first question, but I suppose he's concentrating on keeping the chopper in the air.

"No. The reception was bad. But it's a bit of a coincidence, isn't it? Do you think someone else is looking for the diary?" I suddenly feel a sense of panic. What am I doing? I need to go to the police. If Gillian is really in danger of harming herself, a police chopper would be much more helpful. "Richard, it's not too late. Let's go to the police."

He doesn't respond. He knows more than he's letting on, but there's no point pushing any harder. He's made up his mind.

"Dear God, the very houses seem asleep," he says as we pass over the town. "And all that mighty heart is lying still. All bright and glittering in the smokeless air."

I look at him in surprise. "You've been reading Wordsworth."

"No, love," he replies, his voice soft and melancholic. "Not for many years."

59

JAMES

1 December

I'm sitting in a diner in a small town in Colorado when I get a phone call. It's been weeks since I've heard it ring, and it almost stops before I can find the phone in my pack.

"James Devery?"

"Speaking."

"Kyle Saunders from Dean and Weir. We're a law firm in New York. I'm afraid I have some bad news about your..." He shuffles some papers. "Biological father. I take it the police haven't been in contact?"

A waitress comes over and delivers eggs on toast, sunny side up. It has been my favorite ever since I was a kid.

"Police? No, no. Why? I haven't seen my father in..." The lie trails off. "What is it?"

"I'm afraid he's passed away. I won't go into the details now, but the upshot is that you are the major beneficiary of Mr. Eastman's estate."

"What about his wife?"

I hear him shuffle more papers around. "I'm afraid Victoria Eastman has also passed. I'm sorry, Mr Devery."

I take a bite and close my eyes. I'm in his will. Did that mean he had regrets?

"There is one condition, though. And it's quite a significant one."

Shit—of course there is.

"You have to enroll in the armed services for two years."

I almost choke on my eggs. "Excuse me?"

"Upon successful completion of service, the title to the Eastman Estate and the remainder of assets, currently valued at ten million dollars, will be transferred into your name."

The army—I couldn't think of anything worse. That meant Afghanistan or Iraq. I'd be cannon fodder. Maybe I could test my way into intelligence or something away from the front lines.

"Fine." I push my eggs around my plate. This would disrupt my plans. But the money will save my mother's life. "Was anyone else in the will?"

"I can't name anyone. But Mr. Eastman's other children will also receive a portion of his estate, though you are the primary—"

"Other children?" I say, cutting him off. I remember the preschooler I had seen in the hallway. Is she my sister? And did that mean there were others?

There's an awkward pause. He knows he's said more than he should. "We'll be in touch."

"Wait," I say.

"I have other calls to make, I'm afraid, Mr Devery."

"Just quickly."

"Shoot."

I let the waitress take the remains of my eggs, then stand up. The sun is bright against the winter snow. It's a new day, a new life.

"How do I change my name? I know it sounds strange, but I want to honor my father. I want to become Richard Eastman."

December 2

I touch the naked back beside me. Her name is Alison. She approached me while I was drinking alone at the bar and complimented my eyes. We talked for hours. Her friends laughed from the table behind her, then whistled, and then gave up.

I thought it would help to be with another woman, but when it was all over, I saw I was wrong. When I sleep tonight, I'll dream of her. V. Victoria. If I'm lucky, I'll dream of her alive. Of kissing her, touching her, laughing with her.

But I already know that I won't be lucky.

Tomorrow, I'll see Mother again. I wonder if the death of the Eastmans made it to the news in Texas. I suppose they have enough murders of their own down there.

She'll be happy, though. The prosperity of Richard Eastman was the greatest injustice in my mother's life. They fell in love when they were teenagers, but as soon as Mother fell pregnant and refused to get an abortion, he turned on her.

That's when she found out about the other woman. He was a philanderer—that was one of her names for him. Deadbeat. Asshole. Jackass. When she was in a more reflective mood, he was just a heartbreaker.

When I was younger, I used to create elaborate fantasies about him. I'd pretend that he was in the Marines, fighting Russians overseas. Or that he was a criminal mastermind, stealing rare artifacts from the world's most famous museums.

Mom put a stop to that. When I became a teenager, she told me the whole story. He went away and got rich but never gave her a dime. She had to work two jobs just to keep a roof over our heads. She had to share her bed with a revolving cast of abusers and liars in the hope that one of them could become a proper father to me.

The poverty drove her to the bottle—and, later, much worse.

I wanted to confront him right then, but Mom always refused to tell me anything more about him. She wouldn't even tell me his full name. The older I got, the more furious I became. As Mom cycled through abusive assholes, I blamed my dad for everything. He had the power to give us another life, and he kept it from us.

When I turned eighteen, Mom gave me an envelope with his name and address.

"It's up to you what you do with this," she said. "You can burn it, try to meet him, whatever you want."

"Does he know?" I asked.

"I haven't spoken to the man directly since he left. And you need to understand that he hasn't asked about you either. So don't expect some emotional reunion because I don't think that's on the cards with a man like this. But this is where he lives now." She turned away from me. I remember her holding a cigarette and staring out the window at the dilapidated house next door. The tip of ash grew until, after a minute, it toppled to my bedroom floor.

I opened the envelope and saw "Eastman Estate."

"You said he was rich. How rich are we talking?"

"Rich enough that you should have had a different life." She kept staring out of the window. "Want my advice? Go and get what's owed."

"How?"

She swore as another dusting of ash fell from her cigarette. "You're my brilliant son. You'll find a way."

I stared at her for a moment, then nodded.

"And how much are we owed?"

She turned to face me, and I saw tears in her eyes. She knew exactly what she was doing, what she was asking. And she knew that I would give it to her.

"Everything."

60

VIRGINIA

Richard is unnaturally calm as the helicopter buckles in the wind. The storm has picked up, and I feel like the odds of us landing safely are quickly approaching zero.

"Let's turn back," I say for the third time. But once again, he ignores me. I say a silent prayer and wonder if a helicopter crash is a good way to die. It wouldn't be like a car crash—it would be a quick and violent explosion, efficient and absolute.

We begin to climb, and I see that he's following the line of the road, just visible in the moonlight. I look up at the mountains, which look so steep and severe that they could be from another world.

We shouldn't be here, I think to myself. Humans shouldn't be here. That's what this feeling of terror means.

Leave.

I make out the cabin, faintly lit, the only sign of life on the dark mountainside. But I can't see how Richard is going to land. There's no helicopter pad, and it's impossible to tell what's under the snow in the dark.

But this doesn't stop him. He begins the descent, and all at once, we're rapidly approaching the ground. One wrong move, I think, and we're dead. My stomach lurches like I'm on a rollercoaster. I let out a scream as the chopper jolts violently, but Richard calmly manages to get us steady again. In an instant, we're on solid ground. I tear at my seatbelt and open the door while Richard yells at me to wait, and a second later, I'm vomiting hot bile into the snow.

"Never again," I croak when the chopper is silent.

He nods, then holds out his hand. "Come on. Let's get this over with."

We walk hand in hand to the cabin, which seems to glow like a furnace against the night. As we get closer, I see smoke drifting into the air—she's lit the fire. Given how scared she seemed of Richard, I thought she would run off at the sound of the helicopter. But the snow around the cabin is clean, with no footprints. There's a Mercedes parked outside—my Mercedes.

"What are you going to do?" I ask as we approach the door.

He looks at me with a faint smile on his lips. "End it."

But when we get through the door, the smile fades.

Gillian is sitting in an armchair facing the door, aiming a shotgun at Richard's head.

"You came," she says. "I was wondering how long it would take."

61

GILLIAN

My mother died of lung cancer on the first of July. She was fifty-five years old. There were twenty-seven people at her funeral, which we held in a church. I'd only ever heard Mom speak of God or Jesus when she was cursing me out, though she liked to make the sign of the cross whenever she heard bad news.

The day after her funeral, I put the house on the market. We were in a shit part of a shit town, and after all the bills were paid—the doctors, the estate, the credit cards, the mortgages she had taken out during her many relapses—I had two thousand dollars.

I sold the furniture, the plates, the books. Everything she owned was sold or binned.

It happened so quickly. One day she was a person, taking up space in the world with her body and her possessions. The next, she's just a memory and a plot of land in the graveyard.

When I spoke at her funeral, looking over the small group of friends and acquaintances, I thought, who else will remember her but me? Most of these people hated my mother at one time or another. She was never an easy woman, and the addiction made it so much worse.

For the last seventeen years—my entire life—Mom was on a downward spiral. When I was born, she owned the house freehold and lived with my father. He left when I was five. That's the first time in my life she relapsed.

It happened again when I was nine and again throughout my teenage years. We never had enough money to pay the bills. The power got shut off multiple times a year, which almost killed us during the summer heatwaves. Sometimes, we ate rice and beans every night for weeks on end.

After she died, I wondered if I'd follow in her footsteps. I had no money, no education, no skills.

But then, one day, I saw my way out.

I was standing in my empty bedroom when I noticed that one of the skirting boards was broken. I went down to shove it back into place and saw a cavity in the wall. That was when I found a metal box full of notebooks written by the brother Mom never talked about.

I took them back to the motel I was staying in while the transaction for the house closed. I spent a whole day reading them all. Most of the entries were embarrassing rants about being a teenager; some were graphic depictions of sexual encounters with girls he went to school with. It was after midnight when I came across the final journal.

The story of James and V.

After I finished it, I knew I had my ticket to a different life. With the help of the executor, I tracked down my brother and made my demands. Half his estate. The next day, I received reports from the real estate agent that someone had broken into the house.

I knew it was Richard and that I had to be careful. It wasn't going to be easy, but I wasn't about to give up.

I took the bus to Frostwood and paid for a storage unit on the outskirts of town. I bought a safe and placed the diary there, then walked for hours to the estate. I told the old property manager PJ that I was Richard Eastman's sister, and after a quick phone call, he let me in.

I spent the next few weeks waiting for Richard to make his move.

One day, there was a knock at the door, and I met Steve. He told me that he had just got out of prison and that his ex was married to Richard. We got drunk together that night and ended up in bed. I can admit now that I fell in love with him that night.

We didn't get out of bed for three days straight. On the third night, I told him why I was here. We agreed I needed to move the safe somewhere more private. He searched online until he found a caravan in the woods, and told me he would look after it. We also made our plan to harass Virginia as a way to speed up Richard's decision to sell the estate.

He left on the fourth day. That was the last time I saw him alive.

Four days. Is that enough time to fall in love?

Maybe I'm just a kid, manipulated by an older man. But I don't think so. I think what we had was special. He's the only man I've ever loved.

Not my father. Not my brother.

Just Steve.

And now he's dead. And Richard and the bitch are still alive.

But not for long.

62

VIRGINIA

"Gillian." He says the name slowly as if he'd only just been introduced. "What are you doing?"

"My fallback plan." She stares at him for a moment. "Did you think I wasn't going to fight back?"

Richard shakes his head but doesn't speak.

"Put it down, Gillian," I say. "It's over. This is going to make everything worse."

She snorts as if I were a child who had said something amusingly naive. "No, this is going to solve all my problems. See, I'm Richard's sister. If he dies, I have a claim on his estate. Perhaps a big one."

"What about me?"

"Yes. That's the question, ain't it?" She looks at me and frowns. "You're such a puzzle. At first, I thought you were just some trophy wife I could scare away. But then Steve told me the whole story. You're a killer, just like this asshole."

I feel like time in this room has slowed. Outside, mountains are rising and falling, glaciers are melting, and rivers are forcing their way across new geographies.

Cities burning and rebuilding.

"What do you mean?" I ask.

"She killed someone," she tells Richard, ignoring my question. "Did she not tell you that? It's something you have in common."

"Gillian!" he yells. "Stop this!"

For a second, I'm surprised that he doesn't seem to care about this revelation. When she says I'm a killer, he doesn't even look at me. But when I see the fury in his expression, I suddenly understand what she's trying to say.

"It was you," I whisper to myself. Then, once again, louder. "James."

My husband wrote the diaries.

My husband, his father, and his lover—the true love of his life.

How did I not figure it out sooner? The hate, the drive for revenge and humiliation. I'm an idiot.

But worse: I'm in danger.

I step back until I'm pressed against the wall. Richard and Gillian are both armed, and they both want me dead. There's a chance I can make it to the door, but my only hope is to run down the mountains until I get cell service. Without a winter coat. During a blizzard.

I'm already dead.

"Yes," Richard says, turning to me. "My father abandoned us when I was just a baby. He ran from his responsibilities and left Mom by herself. Then he got rich. But even then, the suffering didn't end. I hated him for years. It was poisoning me. I could feel it in my blood, Virginia. I didn't just want to kill him—I wanted to ruin him for what he'd done to us."

"What about Victoria?"

I don't know what I'm doing. I shouldn't be trying to make him talk. My only thought should be to get off this mountain safely. But the way Gillian looks at Richard, I might not have another chance to get the truth.

"It was the only way. I knew Victoria wouldn't stay strong. If I had let her live, I'd still be in jail—or on death row. I wanted to let her live. I really did."

It's pitch black outside. Maybe time has accelerated all the way to the end of the world. Perhaps the sun has extinguished itself. Maybe the seas have gone still.

Seasonless, herbless, treeless, manless, lifeless. A lump of death —a chaos of hard clay.

"That's very moving," Gillian says, standing up. "But we don't have long. That helicopter probably got some attention. I wouldn't be surprised if someone's on their way." She moves closer to Richard, shaking her head. "It could have been different, you know. If you just gave me what I was owed."

"Walk away," Richard growls. "I can give you money. I could have given you money months ago, easily. But you had to ask for half."

"I deserve half! You left us. Just like your dad left you."

He scowls at the comparison. "I'm not your daddy. I don't owe you shit."

"Yes, you do! Steve was right to push you."

"My Steve?" I ask, causing Richard to wince.

"He was my Steve by the end," Gillian says. There are tears in her eyes. "I loved him. We had a plan. He would look after the safe. And I would make your life unbearable... I figured you'd make him sell, eventually."

"I'll never sell! Do you know what I had to do to get the

estate?" Richard roars, reaching for his gun. Gillian panics and tries to fire, but there's only a click.

"What the..." Gillian says, pulling the trigger again.

"You stole my shotgun," Richard says, wagging his finger at Gillian. "It needs servicing. It hasn't worked in years. It was my father's."

Gillian screams as Richard raises his gun.

"No! Don't do it!" I yell, but he ignores me.

She drops the shotgun and starts to move away—but it's too late. He shoots her in the chest, and she falls to the floor with a sickening moan.

While he walks over to her body to check if she's dead, I make it to the door, and before he can turn and shoot, I'm outside and sprinting into the black snow.

63

JAMES

3 December

The grass in the front yard is up to my knees. I've been away since school ended, and the place has already turned to shit. I mentally add it to the list of maintenance chores I will have to get through.

Mom is jogging up the path when the gate clicks shut behind me. It's mid-morning, and she's still in her robe, but at least she seems sober.

"Hi, Mom." I hug her tight. She's skin and bones, just like always, but she feels like she's aged a decade since I left. "You look pale. Are you looking after yourself?"

"James, it's so good to see you!" Closer up, I can see she's wearing makeup and a floral dress under her robe, but I can also see that she's relapsed since I left. The state paid for her last rehab. I'd hoped it would be her last, but clearly not.

She kisses me on the cheek a few times until I pull away. "Okay, chill!"

I follow her inside with my bag. "Put your stuff in your room, and I'll make coffee."

"Thanks, Mom."

I go down the dark hallway to my tiny room at the back. I feel mildly nauseous as I step inside, as if the air were poisonous. The room is a lie. Basketball and football stars, a few girls in bikinis from a magazine, some photos of parties and ex-girlfriends. I copied all of it from friends at school.

It was never me, and it sickens me now that I've left it behind. This is the room of James, the boy I pretended to be for so long. I want to rip it all down, but I know that'll just lead to her asking questions.

"Coffee's ready!"

"Coming!"

I open my bag and reach in to grab the diary. I should burn it—but it's my only record of her. As the years go by, I'll forget her. But at least I'll have this record of our love. Maybe it's the only real love I'll ever know.

I move my bed as silently as possible and remove a skirting board from the corner of the room. A hollow cavity runs down into the floor, in which a metal box is stored. I open it, and a dozen notebooks spill out. I carefully put them back in order and add the latest—and the last record of James—to the top. I lock the box and carefully put everything back in place.

One day, when I have more time, I'll come back and bury it.

"Just as you like it," she says, giving me a cup that's gone nearly white with creamer.

"Thanks." I sit down at the kitchen table. "Did you see the news?"

"No."

I study her expression, looking for a sign that she's lying. She knows I was there; if she saw the news of their deaths, surely she would have mentioned it by now?

"He's dead."

Coffee slops over the edge of her cup to the filthy linoleum floor. "Richard?"

"And the wife."

She puts down her dripping cup and sits. "Jesus, what a tragedy. How?"

"Police say she shot him, then herself. In that big mansion of his. He'd been stepping out on her."

"No shit." She shakes her head for a moment, then makes the sign of the cross. "And you were staying there?"

I stare at her in disbelief. She's acting like she doesn't know what happened.

"Yes."

"Poor man." She picks up her coffee, stares at it, then puts it back on the table.

"What do you mean? He got what he deserved."

"You're a tough kid," she says, staring into her coffee. "That's your father."

"No father of mine." I slam my fist on the table. "Are you grieving for him? You should be celebrating. He needed killing."

She recoils suddenly and then makes the sign of the cross once again. "What do you mean? Needed killing?"

"Shit, Mom." I lean in, my voice barely above a whisper. "You think it was a coincidence that I was staying there? Why do you think I was there and not at college? I risked everything, and now you sit here pretending—"

"What did you do?" She looks scared. "Did you—"

Before she can finish the question, I hear the screen door slam shut. A second later, a squat bearded man looks me up and down.

"Darling, I told you about..." I'm confused, but then I see that she's talking to the douchebag. "My son James."

The man holds out his hand. "Kyle. Nice to meet you, son."

The word makes me want to vomit. I stare at the hand, then glare at Mother. "Christ, not again."

"James Devery!" Mom looks like she wants to hit me—as does the douchebag. "Can you give us a minute?"

Kyle stares for a moment—his fists are clenched, but it's obviously for show—then goes to the living room.

"It was going to be just us," I complain. "You promised. No more strays."

"It's not that simple, James. You can't expect me to live here alone like a hermit."

"You can come with me."

"This is my home."

"A shitbox in Texas?" The walls in the house are practically made of cardboard. I feel the urge to punch a hole in the wall to make my point.

"It's your home, too." She reaches out to touch my arm, but I jump away as if she's radioactive. "Darling!"

"He's just another waster. He'll pass through and leave your life in pieces. You'll be lucky if he doesn't lay hands on you."

"James Devery!"

"You know I'm right. They're all the same, all the dirtbags wandering through this town."

"Shut your mouth and show some respect. This isn't how

I raised you." She lowers her voice to an angry whisper. "Kyle is in the next room and can hear every damn word you're saying."

"Let me say it to his face, then."

"No." She steps forward and whispers in my ear. "What did you do?"

"What you always wanted. Revenge."

She steps away from me. She looks frightened — the way she looks when one of her strays is losing his temper. "You have to turn yourself in."

I can't believe what I'm hearing. Turn myself in? "This was your idea!"

The door to the kitchen opens, and Kyle pops his head in. "Everything okay?"

Mom flashes him one of her cheesy smiles. "Fine. Just sorting out the boy."

Kyle frowns at me and nods. I can tell he's already sized me up and seen that I'm not someone he can push around. "I'll be having a smoke outside."

"I'll join you soon, darling."

I wince at the word. When the front door shuts, she pushes me in the shoulder. "How dare you? You're evil."

I blink away tears. Evil? "I did this for you, Mom. He ruined our lives."

She waves her hand dismissively. "Nonsense. How do you think I have this house?"

"What?" I feel winded.

"This house. I own it outright. How do you think that happened with eight bucks an hour at the diner? There was nothing when you were little, that's true. But later, when he became a big shot, he gave us some money. Doesn't make him a good man, but he gave us more than the law said he should."

My knees suddenly give way. I'm leaning against the refrigerator, staring down at the peeling linoleum. Two dead and a life of hate—for what?

"Where did all the money go?"

"Darling..." she says, touching my shoulder. I slap her away—and then suddenly, I'm on my feet again.

"Where did it go?" I remember those months in which she was out of work, drunk or high, whenever I got home from school. I thought she was on welfare, but could welfare have ever paid for that habit? "Do you know what I did for you?"

She's backing away, and when she's against the wall, she raises her hands to her face. "I'm pregnant."

I stop moving and let my fists unclench. I suddenly feel empty. Two dead already. No more.

"Pregnant? With that loser?"

"Please. It's your baby sister."

"No," I say, backing away. I'm shaking my head hard like I'm hoping my dark thoughts will fall out and land with a thud on the table. "Not mine."

I walk to the door and see Kyle staring from the back garden. I have an urge to smash his head into the brick path again and again. To watch his life drain away. Is this who I've become?

"Where are you going?"

"Away from here. I have money—or at least, I will soon enough. His whole estate. Did I tell you that?"

Her eyes widen. "Don't leave us," she says. "Don't leave me alone."

"Yeah, I thought that would get your attention."

I open the back door, and she rushes to grab my arm. "We need you. You'll be no better than him."

"No," I say, glaring at her for the last time. "But I'll be a hell of a lot better than trash like you."

64

VIRGINIA

I take a few steps away from the house, then hear another two shots. Richard's finished her off—and I know I'll be next. If I run into the dark, he won't easily find me. The snow is heavy now, and there's no light outside. But I'm already aching from the cold. A few hours in this weather, and I'll be dead.

That leaves one other option. I run to the far side of the Mercedes parked in the driveway and quietly open the back door just as I hear Richard stride out to the deck of the cabin.

"Virginia! I'm not going to hurt you!"

There's a gust of wind, and I use it to close the back door without him hearing.

"Virginia!" he yells. I get as low as I can. For a moment, the car is filled with light from a torch.

I hear his footsteps crunching in the snow. He's getting closer. The light comes back, then away again. I pray the snow has covered my tracks, but I can't be sure. There's a moment of silence, then he moves away.

What am I going to do?

"Virginia!"

He's further away now. Do I wait? Gillian said someone might be coming, but that was speculation.

No—I need to be gone by the time he gets back. And there's only one way that's going to happen.

I wait to hear him call out again, then open the door and tumble out. My legs are frozen, but I do my best to sprint towards the cabin. When I get inside, he calls out again— he's out the back. I have to move fast, but I freeze when I see Gillian's body. Her white top is soaked in crimson. The blood has drained from her head, forming an enormous speech bubble.

I've only seen that much blood once before.

The old man we killed.

No—*I* killed.

"Don't be scared! I won't hurt you!"

Richard's voice is louder now. I run across to Gillian's body.

"I'm so sorry," I whisper as I rummage through her pockets until I find what I need.

The keys to the Mercedes.

As I go back to the front door, I hear his footsteps coming around the side of the house, but it's too late to change course. I leap down the stairs of the deck and sprint across to the car, Richard's footsteps behind me.

Close. Too close.

I open the front door and lock it behind me, but as I fumble with the keys, he slams his shoulder into the window —once, twice, and then it cracks. Before I know it, his hands are on me, the keys are on the floor, and he's pulling me out of the window by my arm and then my hair. Shards of glass are slicing my shoulder and torso as I fly through the air onto the snow.

"Don't fight me," he grunts. He pulls me to my feet and pushes me back towards the cabin. I stumble into the snow again. He pulls me up by the hair, and I scream out in pain and terror. When he pushes me again, I stay on my feet, up the stairs, into the cabin.

I end up a few feet away from Gillian's body.

"Please," I say, my heart racing, my knees weak. There's no hope anymore, but I don't want to die, so I keep talking. "You don't need to do this."

He shakes his head. "Virginia."

"I love you. Please. I'll help you."

"Lies!" He fires his gun just past me, the bullet smashing through the window. "I can't trust you. Just like I couldn't trust her."

"I'm not like her!" I don't know what else to say. "Please."

"You know my sister? The woman you thought I was sleeping with? You know what else she is? An ex-cop. She was helping me do some investigating. Gillian had a tight routine. She only ever went to the town. She never had any contact with your boyfriend, Steve."

"He's not my boyfriend."

"The thing about having a private investigator is that you soon discover other people's lies. After Gillian didn't lead anywhere, I had her run some checks on you. This week, I got some news. I know what you did."

He trails off, and I suddenly feel sick. "You wanted me to be her replacement?"

"You're the spitting image. And with the poetry... even the name was similar. It was part of the attraction." He spits on the ground in disgust. "But it was never the same. You were never like her."

"We were alike in one way," I say.

"What's that?" He's smiling as though he's enjoying this last encounter.

"I read your diary. I saw how she treated you." I force a laugh—a cruel laugh. Before I go, I want to stick the knife in. "It's the same way I treated you. She was in control the whole time. She needed you to escape her life, and so she used you. Just like I used you."

"You don't know what you're talking about!"

I see a movement behind Richard outside.

"You're so naive. Why would either of us go for a man like you? Seriously? Mom was right. You're dead inside."

It's PJ! His face is against the glass. He raises his finger to his lips, and I pray my eyes won't give him away.

"You're just being cruel," he says, shaking his head. "Let's not make this undignified."

I give a loud, unnatural laugh, hoping to give cover to PJ as he opens the door—but as I do so, Richard swings around and fires three times.

"No!" I scream as PJ falls to the floor.

That's it.

All hope is lost.

I close my eyes and whisper a prayer. So many are dead —why not me? Why would I be any different?

I wait for a second. When I open them again, he's standing close to me.

"I didn't tell you the other way Victoria and I were alike," I say, barely above a whisper.

"Go on. Say your last words."

"We never loved you."

I close my eyes tight—but then immediately open them again at the sound of screaming. Richard is swearing while a snarling creature locks its jaws on his right bicep.

Casper! The gun rattles to the ground. I scramble across and pick it up as Richard falls to his knees.

"Down. girl!" I say. Casper looks at me, then gives him one more nip before trotting to my side. With my free hand, I give her a scratch behind the ears.

And then I turn my attention back to Richard, who's trying to stand up.

I want to say the colors were swirling, the ground shifting, my thoughts muddled. But that wasn't it at all. I was calm and clear-headed.

"Bitch!" he yells, and Casper steps towards him, growling.

As he kicks out at the dog, I fire. It hits him in the shoulder, and he falls back to the ground.

"Now, Richard," I say, kneeling to hug Casper close. "Let's not make this undignified."

And then I fire into his body, again and again, until the gun is empty.

65

VIRGINIA

One year later

I throw a stick for the thirty-second time that day, and the collie sprints across the grass. There's no sign that his energy is flagging. PJ had warned me before I took the puppy, but I couldn't help it. If I couldn't have Casper, having her son was the next best thing.

"Good boy, Ghost," I say, attaching his lead and heading out of the dog park. I'd always thought Casper was just overfed, but it turned out she'd been pregnant that whole time. She'd given birth to an entire litter only a few weeks after the death of Richard.

Before I can reach the gate, a man in a crisp white shirt approaches me and smiles.

"What's your dog's name?"

I raise an eyebrow. It's been a while since a man approaches me like this. "Ghost."

"He's beautiful," he says, taking off his sunglasses. The

man looks young and has astonishing green eyes. "But not as beautiful as—"

"Not interested," I say, though I find myself unable to look away.

"Not even for a coffee?"

"Sorry." I feel a twinge of regret. The guy seems corny as hell and about ten years too young for me, but as Mom keeps saying, it's time for me to live again. Why shouldn't I have fun? "I have somewhere to be."

He kneels down, and Ghost licks his face. He smiles and scratches him around the ears. "No kidding, this is a beautiful dog."

Okay. That's all the sign I need. It's time.

"How about I give you my number instead?"

"You made it!"

PJ stands with difficulty, wincing as he pushes on his wooden cane. "Don't," I say, knowing that he won't be stopped. I lean across, hug PJ, and wave for him to sit. "And of course I made it. I live twenty minutes away. You had to fly across the country."

"It's a bit of excitement, seeing the big city." He tugs awkwardly at his blazer. "Don't see much of this in Frostwood."

"Bullshit." I sit and wave at the waitress. "I need a drink."

A few minutes later, I'm sipping on a gin and tonic. PJ takes a large gulp of beer and then begins to rip his napkin into small pieces.

"This is weird, huh?" I say.

"What gives you that idea?"

I laugh and then lean forward. "I know you don't want to hear it, but thank you. I'd be dead without you."

"No need." He shakes his head vigorously. "You saved my life too, remember? He'd have finished me off, no question."

"It's not the same."

"Hell it isn't." We're quiet for a moment, and then both burst out laughing. "I didn't come here for that. This is a celebration. We're survivors."

"Hell yeah." I down my drink and wave for another. "But what you did in court—"

"Hush now."

"You—"

"I'm serious, Virginia. I'm going to walk out that door!"

I lean back in my chair and smile. I can still remember the interviews with the police. We didn't have long to get our stories straight, and they tripped me up with contradictions more than once. But in the end, a confession is a confession, and the fact that PJ was almost killed made the charge of self-defense easy to accept.

Ultimately, I'm not sure the detectives believed our story. But the fact that Richard had murdered Gillian and Steve in cold blood and already shot PJ meant that they were happy enough to close out the case.

"I'd probably be in prison right now," I ventured. "Maybe for the rest of my life. With my history..."

PJ made a show of trying to stand up with his cane, then relaxed back into his chair. "You're lucky it's such a pain to walk with this bum leg." After Richard had shot him in the chest and thigh, PJ suffered nerve damage, which meant he would always walk with a cane. "But you're welcome. You've more than paid me back."

"It's just money."

"I would have preferred the land."

I almost choke on my drink. This had been the one sore point with the distribution of Richard's estate. I'd given PJ five million in cash to make up for what his father had lost. But the land had gone to Simone and her tribe.

"Her people were there first."

"Let's change the subject," he replies with a roll of his eyes. "How's your mom?"

"Annoying as hell."

"She's not grateful you paid off her house?"

My phone vibrates on the table. I flip it over and read the text.

Dinner tonight? Adam from the park :).

"Folks are a bit rude in the city," PJ mutters.

"Sorry, sorry." I flip the phone back over, then finish my drink in one go. "Mom's gratitude lasted about a week. Now she's on my case to move out."

PJ raises an eyebrow. "You're a rich single woman with no commitments. The lady has a point."

Now, it's my turn to roll my eyes. "Not you, too."

"I'm serious, young lady. You need to live."

"Yeah." Despite the drink, I still feel sober—too sober to have this conversation. "It's been hard."

Next to us, a man in a suit talks quietly to a woman in a black dress. She's in heels, one tucked behind her ankle. I imagine he works in finance or tech, and she's a lawyer. This is probably their only break before finishing work at 8 p.m. They're a beautiful couple, though. Lean, manicured, shiny. Richard and I were like that once.

"Have there been..." he trails off, but I know what he's

trying to ask. Have there been any psychotic breaks? Have you lost your marbles? Are you sane?

"I'm talking to someone. It's helping." He raises an eyebrow but doesn't respond. But I know what he's thinking. I killed my husband in cold blood. I could have waited for the police to arrive, but I didn't. That's hardly a sign of perfect mental health. "What about you?"

"It's just me and Casper on the land. I'm helping out the colonizers next door."

The joke is in bad taste, but I can't help smiling. "You should talk to someone."

"I like being alone."

"That's not what I mean."

We chat for another hour, and then I help PJ to his feet and walk him to a cab. He's returning to his hotel and, apparently, to a Broadway show.

"It's time I broadened my horizons," he says as he gets inside the taxi. "Maybe you should do the same."

"Shut up, old man," I say with a grin. "Till next time."

I wave as the taxi drives off, then take my phone out and send a reply to Adam. PJ's right. I'm rich, single, and relatively young. Why not live my life?

Sure. What did you have in mind?

66

ADAM

While Virginia sleeps in the bedroom, I walk over to the window and look down at the Hudson. I'm wearing a robe around my naked body with the letters 'R.E.' sewn into the wool.

This is his apartment.

I'm here. Finally.

I was surprised when she said we should come here. For the last week, I'd followed her back to her mother's house in Queens, and I figured that was all she had. I'd even booked a fancy hotel room, just in case.

When she told me this was her ex-husband's place, I knew it was meant to be. They had lived here as man and wife before moving to Montana.

Montana was where I met Virginia for the first time, not that she remembers me. I was just the builder's apprentice. Since then, I've dyed my hair and grown a beard.

In fact, tonight wasn't even the first time she'd seen me naked.

Over dinner, I thought there were a few glimmers of

recognition. But Virginia couldn't possibly guess who I really was. I told her I was twenty-five and a junior analyst on Wall Street, which she believed. The reality is that I had only just celebrated my eighteenth birthday.

After dinner, we walked through the park, and she told me fragments of her life. She claimed to be a divorced communications consultant looking for a new career. I told her I was looking for something new.

"Everyone sleepwalks through life, don't you think?" I said, stopping to look over the lake. "I don't want that to be my life."

"I don't know," she murmured. "I've had enough drama for a while."

"No drama. Just meaning." I took her hand. "To me the meanest flower that blows can give thoughts that do lie too deep for tears."

She looked at me with curiosity. "You like Wordsworth?"

"It was a gift from my father," I replied shyly. "I memorized a few things to seduce women."

At this, she laughed. And then she kissed me.

My big worry was that I wouldn't be able to do it—that my hate for this woman would make it impossible. But when we kissed, I genuinely wanted her. It scared me, but not enough to put me off the plan. It must be genetic, I think to myself, this love of slender brunettes.

"I hate to admit it, but it's working," she said, running her hands over my abdominals. "Do you have any other lines for me?"

"Just that you're beautiful," I said, kissing her again.

"That's weak sauce," she whispered in my ear after pulling away.

"But?"

She waved at me to follow her, and soon, we were in a cab heading to her apartment.

And that was it. After months of planning, I succeeded on my first try. All those days spent following her movements, learning everything about her, planning a series of dates to lure her onto the line—and she was already hooked!

It didn't have to be like this. All I wanted was to know my father. Mom had known his name my entire life. They were only together that one night, but when she fell pregnant, she tried her best to find him. She eventually discovered that he had gone off to do a tour in Iraq.

Later, she met a new man and married him. He was Dad —the only dad I ever knew. But I always felt the absence of my real father, and from a young age, I would hound my mom to help me find him.

On my sixteenth birthday, she relented and gave me his name and location. Richard Eastman from Montana. I followed a few dead ends before showing Mom some photos of people on LinkedIn—and she recognized him immediately. He was an executive at GSP New York, a global engineering firm. I spent weeks finding out everything I could about him.

I had planned to meet him in New York, but when I called his office, I discovered he had moved across the country. When I mentioned Montana, the secretary confirmed that he had moved there for the winter.

From there, it was easy. I got a job as an apprentice in the renovation of the mansion on his estate, and after a few days, I gathered the courage to approach him. I was prepared to be rejected, but when I told him about my mother, he immediately wanted to get to know me. That first weekend, he took me on a hunting trip into the mountains. He promised to bring me to New York when the house was finished—but said he had a problem to deal with first.

I didn't mind. We had our whole lives ahead of us.

The work on the mansion was slow, but we got to see each other most weekends. On the days that he was busy, I explored the property. One day, two girls approached me and asked if I wanted a drink. The blonde introduced herself as Gillian and explained that she was a relative of Richard Eastman. The redhead was quiet at first—but after a few drinks, she was all over me.

When it got dark, Gillian led us to the house, saying that Richard and his wife were out for the night. We drank some more, and then Gillian disappeared, and it was just me and the redhead. She still hadn't told me her name, but before I knew it, we were in bed together. She was wild, louder than anyone I'd ever been with. When Virginia walked in on us, I felt humiliated. It was only then that I realized that I'd been set up. Gillian had been using me in some strange battle with her brother's wife.

The discovery sent me into a spiral. If Richard found out, he'd be so disgusted that our relationship might never recover.

I thought about leaving. But the next day at work, the foreman told me that Richard Eastman and his sister Gillian were dead. The newspapers said that he had been killed in self-defense, but I didn't believe a word of it. The kind man that had accepted me immediately, without question, couldn't possibly be a murderer.

When the police announced that they weren't pressing charges, I knew I had to act. I saved all my money and hired a private investigator, who got me access to the police files.

My dad's apparent killer had been unconscious when the

police found him—a dozen feet away from the body and the murder weapon. Even stranger, he had his gun, which hadn't been fired that night.

The only prints on the murder weapon, aside from my father's, were hers.

Virginia Eastman's.

He confessed, and the police accepted his bullshit story. She got away with murder, and they both got rich.

For now, anyway. But not for long.

I walk back to the bedroom. She's still asleep.

Father, rest in peace, I whisper to myself. *I'll soon get revenge on the woman who killed you.*

THANK YOU FOR READING

Did you enjoy reading *The Makeover*? Please consider leaving a review on Amazon. Your review will help other readers to discover the novel.

ABOUT THE AUTHOR

Matt McGregor is a writer of psychological thrillers from New Zealand. Before becoming a writer, Matt taught English (briefly), ran a nonprofit, worked with maps, and led a marketing team for a tech startup. Now, he mostly spends his time inventing surprising ways to murder his characters, which is totally fine and nothing for you to worry about. When he's not writing in the third person, he likes to explore the local wilderness, swim in the sea, and play with his exhaustingly energetic young children.

Visit Matt on his website: https://mattmcgregor.co/

ALSO BY MATT MCGREGOR

Made in United States
Cleveland, OH
10 June 2025

17600818R00176